The Gospel of Gollum

Ethical and Mystical Faces in Tolkien's Middle-earth

Ivano Sassanelli

Cover Image © Jay Johnstone 2024

English Translation © Ivano Sassanelli 2025
Text © Ivano Sassanelli 2025

"Tolkien e il vangelo di Gollum" first published in Italian
by Cacucci Editore, Bari 2020.

First published in English by Luna Press Publishing, Edinburgh, 2025

The right of Ivano Sassanelli to be identified as the Authors of the Work has been asserted by each of them in accordance with the Copyright, Designs and Patents Act 1988.

The Gospel of Gollum © 2025. All rights reserved. No part of this publication may be reproduced, stored in a retrieval system, or transmitted in any form or by any means, electronic, mechanical, photocopy, recording or otherwise, without prior written permission of the publisher. Nor can it be circulated in any form of binding or cover other than that in which it is published and without similar condition including this condition being imposed on a subsequent purchaser.

www.lunapresspublishing.com

ISBN-13: 978-1-915556-55-4

"l'amor che move il sole e l'altre stelle"
(Dante Alighieri, Paradiso, XXXIII, v. 145).

Contents

Foreword - Giuseppe Pezzini vii
Introduction ix
Acknowledgments xiii

Chapter 1 - Gollum: The *Monstrum* and The Critics 1
1. The life of Gollum between 'journeys' and 'mirages' 1
2. The *Monstrum* and the Critics 5
    2.1 Woodrow (Woody) and Susan Wendling...5
    2.2 Vito Fascina 9
    2.3 Andrea Monda 10
    2.4 Verlyn Flieger 12
    2.5 Tom Shippey 12
    2.6 Roberto di Scala 14
    2.7 Gollum and other characters of world literature 15
        2.7.1 Lisa Hopkins 15
        2.7.2 Charles Keim 17
        2.7.3 Stefano Giorgianni 20
    2.8 Lucia Opreanu.. 21
    2.9 Yvette Kisor 24
3. Voices in the Darkness: Gollum between Cinema and Dubbing..26
    3.1 Characteristics of the 'voice of Gollum' 27
    3.2 J.R.R. Tolkien: Gollum as read by his creator 28
    3.3 Andy Serkis 29
    3.4 Francesco Vairano 30

Chapter 2 - Gollum and *The Hobbit* 35
Introduction 35
1. *The Hobbit*: A Children's Tale? 36
2. The heart of *The Hobbit* and 'the Gospel of Gollum'.................38
3. The 'first' and 'second' Gollum in *The Hobbit* 42
    3.1 Gollum in the first edition of *The Hobbit* 43

3.2 Gollum in the second edition of *The Hobbit* 46
   3.2.2 Gollum, Bilbo and the Ring of Power 49
4. 'Riddles in the Dark': the renewal ethics of Fairy-stories
and the solitude of an ignoble prisoner 51
   4.1 Bilbo Baggins: a "light out of the past" for Gollum 52
   4.2 "Sun on the Daisies": when riddles solve a human mystery 53
5. Gollum's grandmother: the most important female
memory in Middle-earth 57

Chapter 3 - Gollum and *The Lord of The Rings* 63
1. The narrative genesis of Gollum and Sméagol in
The Lord of the Rings 63
2. Sméagol or Gollum: which character in Tolkien's works? 68
3. Gollum: a journey full of changes 71
4. Gollum, Frodo and Sam: from a 'stealth touch'
to a 'warm caress' 74
   4.1 A 'stealthy touch' in the debate between Sméagol and Gollum
in the slag hole 76
   4.2 An 'affectionate caress' in front of Shelob's lair 80
5. Gollum: the ignoble 'sought', 'pursued' and 'found'
by Pity and Mercy 84
   5.1 Gollum and Bilbo: between Pity and Mercy 86
   5.2 Gollum and Frodo: a relationship of pity, mercy
and forgiveness of injury 91
   5.3 Gollum and Sam: from hatred to compassion 96
   5.4 Gollum and Faramir: a look at justice softened by mercy 97
      5.4.1 Sméagol and his master: an apparent and saving deception ...97
      5.4.2 Gollum being judged by Faramir: between 'equity'
and '*aequitas canonica*' 98
6. The events at the Crack of Doom 103
   6.1 Frodo's failure and Mount Doom: between 'catastrophe',

'eucatastrophe' and 'dyscatastrophe' 104
6.2 Mount Doom and the '*Deus absconditus*' 108
6.3 "Nine-Fingered Frodo": the meaning of being 'incomplete' 112
6.4 Gollum and the events at the Crack of Doom 117
6.5 The last forgiveness for Gollum 120
7. *Post scriptum*: a hypothetical and alternative ending
for Gollum..122

Conclusion 125
Afterword - Oronzo Cilli 130

Bibliography 132

Foreword

Giuseppe Pezzini
Associate Professor of Latin Language and Literature
Fellow and Tutor, Corpus Christi College – University of Oxford

> Grasp the life of man complete!
> Everyone lives, though it's seldom confessed,
> And wherever you grasp, there's interest.
> In varied pictures there's little light,
> A lot of error, and a gleam of right,
> So the best of drinks is brewed,
> So the world's cheered and renewed.
> (J.W. Goethe, *Faust*, Prelude, 167-173)

As in real life, so in great literature there's interest wherever you grasp, and this is certainly true for the world (sub-)created by Tolkien, where every single detail (name, character, scene or tale) is like a rabbit hole that has not yet been fully explored – and indeed will never be, as its borders and dimensions are enlarged at any new exploration. This was the approach that was first followed by Tolkien himself, who can properly be considered as the first explorer of his *legendarium*: as he claimed in several letters, in writing his books he did not invent anything, but rather 'encountered' and 'discovered' on the way, including above all his characters and their significance. This was clearly the case for Gollum, whose narrative depth was not "fully envisaged at first", but "was implicit, and merely needed attention" (*Letters,* Letter 155, 297) and who only gradually "develope[d] into a most intriguing character" (Letter 70, 117).

This booklet is a passionate and learned report of an investigation into the character of Gollum, conducted by an author with interests and expertise in theological matters, but with the intelligence and openness to engage with different approaches (which in my view are all correct and all partial, as in all of them there is "little light […] and a gleam of right"). This is evident especially in the first chapter, which is essentially a comprehensive review of the variety of past explorations into the rabbit hole of this central Tolkienian character, also including his reception in films (and rightly so). In the next chapters we hear more the voice of Sassanelli, who reconstructs the development of Gollum in *The Hobbit* (chapter 2) and *The Lord of the Rings* (chapter 3), providing fresh and insightful analyses of key scenes (including, especially, the Riddle-game and the events at the Cracks of Doom). The discussion is enhanced and enriched in particular by Sassanelli's perceptive decision to shed light on the depths of Gollum's personality by focussing on his relationship with other characters (including his grandmother). The book concludes with a short epilogue in which Sassanelli construes Gollum's character as a special lens through which Tolkien expressed (or explored) his theological insights on mercy and the eucatastrophe, while rightly stressing that, in doing so, "Tolkien did not close himself in tradition but, on the contrary, presented his readers with a world of new meaning". I can promise that 'new meaning' will also be the gift presented to the readers of this unpretentious but well-brewed study, and that their appreciation of Tolkien's literary world will also be "cheered and renewed".

Introduction

Why 'The Gospel'?

The Gospel of Gollum may seem like an unusual title for a text about fantastic literature. What does Gollum have to do with the Gospel? The investigation that will be covered in this book tries to answer this question in two ways.

The first path was an unexpected revelation many years ago. The question I asked myself was: how could Tolkien as a man, Catholic, and writer, have constructed the character of Gollum as a possible exemplification or personification of the passage from the Gospel of Luke: "For where your treasure is, there also will your heart be" (Lk 12:34)?

The second avenue will mainly focus on the possible existence of a 'gospel' – or *evangelium* – that belongs to Gollum in terms of his story's 'message' and 'announcement'.

In order to investigate these two avenues of inquiry, it is necessary to clarify an issue that has gripped Tolkien scholars for several decades and which concerns the relationship between Tolkien's works and his Catholic faith. In fact, literary and theological criticism has often dealt with Tolkien's religious themes within the question of whether the Professor's works were 'pagan' or 'Christian' or the reflection of Tolkien's 'catholicity' in his writings.

Some scholars have questioned, for example, whether the Professor's stories concern a "pre-Christian world" – almost in the context of a *praeparatio evangelii* (Shippey, 2005) – or a "pagan world but in harmony with Christianity" (Testi, 2018).

Tolkien didn't use the adjectives 'pagan' or 'Christian' to describe his works but, as he himself stated in letter n. 142 of 2nd December 1953 (see Sassanelli, 2023b), addressed to his Jesuit friend Father Robert Murray: "*The Lord of the Rings* is of course a fundamentally religious and Catholic work" (Tolkien, 2006c, 172).

Tolkien's literature can rightly be called a "divine narrative" (Pezzini, 2019) or a narrative '*De vera religione*' having at its centre the essential conflict over "God and divine honors" (Tolkien, 2006c, 243), in which the presence of the 'religious' – i.e. the dialogue between 'natural' and 'supernatural' – is continuous, although in many cases not directly and explicitly perceptible. Tolkien, in the pages of his books, makes Eru and the Valar act in a 'hidden' way, not invasive and intrusive but always respectful of their freedom, the characters and his contemporary readers (201). This is why Eru is spoken of as a real "*Deus absconditus*" (Sassanelli, 2023a).

Secondly, Tolkien's works draw on the 'Catholic' source that derives from his religious faith. Sometimes it is on a corrective course, other times in union and harmony with the other sources from his linguistic studies and literary passions (Cilli, 2023). These bones of the ox, then, enter the cauldron of the story and the soup that is served by the author.

Finally, thanks to his intense life as a Christian-Catholic, Tolkien was able to investigate the relationship between the 'Great Eucatastrophe' (i.e. the Birth, Death and the

Resurrection of Christ) which took place in the Primary World and recounted in the Gospels, and the 'eucatastrophe' present in his Secondary World (i.e. the unexpected and joyful reversal contained in Fairy-tales). The *Evangelium* has not abrogated the legends but 'hallowed' them; they contain the eucatastrophic essence, that is, a glow of light, an *evangelium* of Joy beyond the walls of the world.

This sanctification can unfold in two directions: on the one hand, it transforms the 'ennobling' of the hero into a 'sanctification' of the humble (Tolkien, 2006c, 237) and the ignoble for which the intervention of an 'external power' and a 'supernatural and sanctifying grace' is necessary. On the other hand, it can provoke the sanctity present in any reader who approaches such research with an open mind and heart.

The act of sub-creating fantastic stories and tales is a gift given to humankind by that God who, in the Primary World, is at the same time the Creator of all things and the Author of the Word's Incarnation.

Thus, in Tolkien's fantastic literature, the *divine Logos* and the *human verbum* met in that liminal zone between reality and fantasy, mythology and history, legends and the Gospel, which is called 'eucatastrophe'.

Acknowledgments

First of all, I want to thank my family who supported me in this new publishing adventure.

Secondly, special thanks go to Giuseppe Pezzini and Oronzo Cilli for their friendship, courtesy and availability for agreeing to write the Foreword and Afterword to this book.

Also, many thanks to Francesca Barbini and Luna Press Publishing for having faith in my work and for fostering Italian Tolkien scholarship abroad.

Finally, I would like to thank Jay Johnstone for creating the cover art, which I consider a true masterpiece of infinite beauty and artistic depth.

Chapter 1

Gollum: The Monstrum and The Critics

1. The life of Gollum between 'journeys' and 'mirages'

The first step in understanding Gollum is analysing his life and history. From this path we will realise how he was a restless Hobbit, constantly looking for something or someone: he was always on the move, torn between the need to travel – to escape from an enemy or find a refuge – and the incessant desire to find a precious and desirable object that could satisfy him. Therefore, Gollum's life was complex: an adventure made up of 'journeys' and 'mirages'.

From *Appendix B*, 'The tale of years (chronology of the Westlands)', of *The Lord of the Rings* (Tolkien, 2005, 1082-1095) the reader discovers that in about 1150 of the Third Age of Middle-earth, the Stoors – an ancient Hobbit race to which Gollum belonged to – passed the Redhorn pass and settled in Dunland, which some of them abandoned in 1356, returning to Wilderland.

In 1601, many Periannaths (Hobbits) emigrated from Bree, receiving a gift from Argeleb II of the lands beyond the Baranduin and, in about 1630, they were joined by the Stoors from Dunland.

While out fishing on Sméagol's birthday – who would become Gollum – in 2463, his cousin, Déagol, found the One Ring. Longing for it and wanting it as a birthday present, Sméagol killed Déagol. Seven years later, in 2470, he hid deep in the Misty Mountains and began to live a life of darkness, hiding in solitude.

It was in those Mountains much later, in 2941, that Bilbo Baggins, a Hobbit of the Shire, on his way to the Lonely Mountain of Erebor together with Gandalf and some Dwarves led by Thorin Oakenshield, by chance came across Sméagol-Gollum.

The Hobbit won the Ring from the Stoor at the end of a riddle contest and escaped his wrath. From that moment, Gollum chose to take revenge on Bilbo and the entire Baggins family, who had stolen his 'Preciousss'.

Three years later, in 2944, Gollum left the Mountains in search of the 'thief' of the Ring and then, in 2951, turned towards Mordor, where Sauron had begun to rebuild the Tower of Barad-dûr. He arrived there around 2980 and met Shelob, a huge and evil female Spider.

Here, in the late 2000s and early 3000s of the Third Age, Gollum was captured and tortured by Sauron to find out where the One Ring was. In 3017, Gollum was freed from the power of Mordor and, after being found in the Dead Marshes by Aragorn – who, with Gandalf, had been on his trail for years – was led by Thranduil into Mirkwood.

From here, Gollum managed to escape on 20th June 3018. In August that year, it was believed that, being pursued by both the Elves and the servants of Sauron, Gollum had taken refuge in Moria and that, once he discovered the way that led to the West-gate, he would never be able to get out.

In fact, just as the Fellowship of the Ring entered Moria on 13th January 3019, Gollum began following another Hobbit: Frodo Baggins, the Ring-bearer.

After stopping for some time in Lothlórien with Lady Galadriel, the members of the Fellowship departed on 16th February. Gollum followed them, having seen their departure from a hiding place on the western bank of the river.

After the division of the Fellowship of the Ring, when Frodo decided to continue his journey with only Samwise Gamgee on 29th February 3019, the two Hobbits met Gollum in Emyn Muil.

Once captured by Frodo and Sam, Gollum became their guide and promised to lead them to the Black Gate of Mordor. Thus began their adventure, crossing the Dead Marshes on 2nd March, and, two days later, the slag-mounds on the edge of the Desolation of the Morannon.

After meeting Faramir on 7th March, Frodo and Sam were taken to Henneth Annûn, where Gollum was subsequently captured for trespassing. The Stoor was tried by Faramir and, although convicted, was freed thanks to Frodo's benevolent intercession. The next day, he was able to leave with the other two Hobbits. At dusk on 9th March, Frodo, Sam, and Gollum reached the Morgul-road, passing the Cross-roads on the 10th, and witnessing the Morgul army leave Minas Morgul.

On 11th March, Gollum visited Shelob to implement his evil plan against the two Hobbits. But, on that same day, an event occurred that could have changed his life definitively: he watched Frodo and Sam sleeping and felt a flood of emotion and repentance that had been dormant until that moment. Because of his affection for Frodo, he made a sweet gesture towards him, a caress. But Sam's abrupt reaction, who in the meantime had woken up, led Gollum to decide to definitively betray Frodo and lead him to his death in order to recover the Ring.

As a result, Frodo was almost killed by Shelob the next day. But Shelob was defeated and put to flight by Sam. Gollum, meanwhile, managed to escape. Thus, Frodo was kidnapped by the Orcs and taken to Cirith Ungol where, on 14th March, Sam – thanks to the use of the Ring, which he had previously taken possession of – managed to free his Master. The next day, the two Hobbits began their journey north along the Morgai.

Between 18th and 24th March, Frodo and Sam were joined by the Orcs on the road from Durthang to Udûn. Fleeing, they began their long and tiring march on the Barad-dûr road, which they left shortly afterwards to head east towards Mount Doom.

On 25th March, Frodo and Sam reached the Sammath Naur, the Crack of Doom, to throw the One Ring into the fires where it had been forged by Sauron so many years before. However, Gollum was waiting for them, and in an extreme attempt to regain the Ring, he threw himself onto Frodo. He snatched Frodo's finger which the Ring was on and bit it off. Overwhelmed by his exhilaration and joy, Gollum bounded, tripped, and fell into the blazing fires of Mount Doom. He cried out his last word, the name of that which was dearest to him: his 'Preciousss'.

Thus, Gollum's existence ended. He had lived an apparently miserable, desperate life, full of journeys. In Gollum's life, the 'journey' was confused with the 'mirage' of being able to reappropriate an object which, in reality, had always used him for the sole purpose of returning to Sauron, its only Master.

On that late March day, Gollum died, no longer obsessed with the evil Ring that had gifted him a centuries-long life, yet taken everything else away from him.

2. The *Monstrum* and the Critics

Before tackling the analysis of Tolkien's texts about Gollum, it is important to see how this old Hobbit has been analysed and understood by critics of Tolkien's works. In this paragraph, only some readings and opinions by different authors will be discussed in order to show, as an example, how multifaceted and complex Gollum is. He has even aroused divergent and sometimes antithetical opinions.

Even before falling into the category of 'monster', Gollum can be qualified as a *monstrum*, in the Latin sense of the word. In fact, he is a portentous and exceptional phenomenon who goes beyond the limits of normality.

In Tolkien's works, Gollum is a *unicum* (unique): various elements are concentrated in him, including everything that has been analysed in the field of phenomenology and contemporary philosophy with the expression of the "grotesque body" (Bracco, 2016, 63-86).

2.1 Woodrow (Woody) and Susan Wendling: Gollum and the riddle of his name

It is essential to begin with Woodrow (Woody) and Susan Wendling's article, "The Riddle of Gollum: A speculative Meditation on Tolkien's Sources" (Wendling, 2012, 1-7).

The authors tried to reconstruct and trace the origins of the name 'Gollum'. In their analysis, they started from what Tolkien said about the Ents (1), that they were the Shepherds of the Trees and were composed of "philology, literature, and life" (Tolkien, 2006c, 212). According to the authors, this could also be applied to Gollum.

Starting from this conviction, W. and S. Wendling underlined the points of contact between Gollum and the protagonist of the poem *Glip*, which Tolkien had written in 1928 within a series of poems entitled *Tales and Songs of Bimble Bay*.

Through the analysis of this poem, the authors have highlighted the similarities between Glip and Gollum as described in *The Hobbit*. For example, the place where Glip lived was a stone cave and his lair could be considered a mortal place as boats, attracted by the song of the sirens, crashed against the rocks. Like Gollum, also Glip was invisible, his eyes shone with a green light and his voice emitted a high-pitched sound. Finally, in Tolkien's poem, there is a mention of gold rings worn by sirens (Wendling, 2012, 1-2).

The authors reviewed six different literary sources that could have led Tolkien to construct both Gollum's character and name.

The earliest source, according to Wendling and Wendling, may have been the Old Norse word: 'gold' (*Old Norse Gold*) (2-3). This theory is also supported by Douglas A. Anderson in *The Annotated Hobbit*, during his discussion of the meaning of the ancient Norwegian word 'gull/goll', which 'gollum' could be a declension of and could mean either "gold, treasure, something precious" or "ring" (in Tolkien, 2017a, 134).

The second source may have been the Hebrew word 'Golem', which derives from an expression present in verse 16 of Psalm 139 of the Old Testament: "Your eyes say my unformed substance" (Ps 139: 16). According to the authors, the root of the Hebrew word that translates into 'substance' are the consonants GLM. Tolkien had a particular interest in Hebrew and he could have been inspired as much by this biblical verse as by the Jewish legend of the Golem, which tells of a clay creature built to represent a human being, endowed with life but not a soul. This legend also protected Jews locked up in Ghettos. The similarities between Gollum and the Jewish Golem are that both are creatures of the earth; imperfect beings who could become invisible and whose magical powers could be deactivated (Wendling, 2012, 3).

Alongside the Golem, Woody and Susan Wendling also included Frankenstein's monster, as described in Mary Shelley's novel *Frankenstein, or the Modern Prometheus* as a possible source for Tolkien's stories. They underline how literary critics are divided on whether or not the author knew the Jewish legend of the Golem. However, they are equally convinced that there are many similarities to the Monster and Gollum. In fact, according to the authors, the words 'miserable' and 'wretched' are used for the Monster, Frankenstein, and Gollum. Furthermore, both the Monster and Gollum beg their masters for mercy. Finally, the authors also noted the similarity between the creation of Frankenstein's Monster and that of the Uruk-hai by Saruman (3).

Other hypothetical sources concern the term 'Golgotha', i.e. the name of the mountain where Jesus died. According to the authors, it resonates with the essence of the caves in the Misty Mountains in which Gollum lived. Woody and Susan Wendling have also traced a parallelism between Bilbo's duel with Gollum and the biblical story of the conflict between David and 'Goliath' (3).

Furthermore, referring to Tolkien's letters (Tolkien, 2006c, 341) and essay "On Fairy-stories", the authors hypothesised that 'Gorbo' or 'Golithos' – i.e. two protagonists of *The Marvelous Land of Snergs* written in 1928 by Wyke-Smith

– may have been the basis of Gollum's name and character (Wendling, 2012, 4).

Another possible source could have been *The Golliwog Books* (a series of children's stories published between 1895 and 1909 that Tolkien probably knew from his childhood). However, during the Twentieth Century, the word 'golliwog' began to designate 'grotesque black dolls' or 'grotesque people'.[1] Woody and Susan Wendling noted a possible similarity between the meaning of this term and the 'grotesqueness' of Gollum. They also highlighted the phonetic similarity between 'golliwog', 'pollywog', and 'scalawag', emphasising the fact that Gollum was a kind of aquatic creature and a scoundrel (4).

The penultimate source is perhaps one of the most important and attested among those cited: that is, 'Grendel' from *Beowulf*, one of the literary works the Professor most loved and studied. Indeed, a year before *The Hobbit* was published, Tolkien wrote and delivered the lecture, *Beowulf: The Monsters and the Critics* (Tolkien, 2006a, 5-48). This suggests that the two texts influenced each other. The authors emphasise that, without Grendel, Gollum would not have existed. For them, Tolkien believed that his stories were, in reality, true stories, preserved for a long time in the oral tradition and resurfaced in the more recent literature. While on the one hand they claim that Grendel acted as a source for Gollum, on the other hand they argue that, in the mind of the Professor, Gollum was Grendel's source because he was the 'original type' of the character (Wendling, 2012, 4).

---

1. *The Random House Dictionary of the English Language*, 2nd ed., New York: Random House, 1987, cited in Wendling 2012.

The last source is the reference to 'mercy' in The Christian Gospel that is repeatedly expressed in the Catholic mass at the moment of the initial penitential act in which there is the *Kyrie eleison*. Woody and Susan Wendling also focus on the possibility that the name 'Gollum' could be compared to the acronym "GOD Loves U(You) Mercifully!". Therefore, Tolkien would have thought Gollum a sinner, a 'fallen Hobbit' who needed the Pity and Mercy of God (5).

2.2 Vito Fascina: Gollum and Judas

In "'Avanti e in alto. Insieme': percorsi tolkieniani d'inizio secolo" (2021), Vito Fascina analysed how, within Tolkien's works, there is a Merciful Father waiting to lovingly embrace his lost creatures again.

Fascina examines the character of Gollum in the light of Judas's human experience and faith. According to this interpretation, Gollum was free to love until the end but let himself be seduced and captured by the separator – the Devil. For Fascina, it is interesting that Judas was defined, on the one hand, as "guide" ("ὁδ–ηγός") (Acts 1:16) by the evangelist Luke in the Acts of the Apostles and, on the other, as "consignor" ("παραδιδούς") in the Gospel of John (Jn 18:5). Fascina saw a similarity here with Gollum, who played a decisive, and involuntary, role in the salvation of mankind in Tolkien's texts (Fascina, 2021, 81).

Continuing with this parallelism, the author underlined how, in John 13: 26-30, Judas has the possibility of freeing himself from temptation, but prefers to be separated from the Love of God. On the other hand, according to Fascina, at the end of *The Lord of the Rings*, Gollum's closing cry of

"My Preciousss" leaves the reader in a state of suspended judgement about his fate. This expression of joy and fulfilled desire might have been a cry both to the Ring, which Gollum had finally retrieved, and also to a surprisingly merciful gaze that could have passed across him at the moment of his fall into the fires of Mount Doom (81-82).

Fascina identified a two-way contest between the disarmed *alter Christus* and the ignoble, between Frodo and Gollum. However, both appear unsuitable for the role in its highest essence. He wondered if there is in fact a third protagonist in the narrative who, at the same time, is a silent and tenacious *primus agens*, acting through and alongside common and simple Hobbits, pushing them on a fantastic adventure (82).

2.3 Andrea Monda: Gollum as 'alter Frodo' and 'alter Christus'

Andrea Monda thoroughly studied Gollum in three of his books: *L'Anello e la Croce. Significato teologico de Il Signore degli Anelli* (2008); *A proposito degli hobbit* (2013); *J.R.R. Tolkien. L'imprevedibilità del bene* (2021).

In these books, Monda traced the following fundamental themes:

a) The loss of the name;
b) The relationship between Gollum and Frodo;
c) Gollum's death and Christ's sacrifice.

The story of Sméagol, marked by the betrayal and murder of his cousin, as well as his only friend, scarred the Hobbit in such an indelible way as to make him physically and morally ugly (Monda, 2008, 119). At that point, his new name, 'Gollum', no longer made sense to others and was for himself a sign of mockery, a perpetual reminder of his mutterings and gurgles, made in the solitude of his thoughts, full of resentment and anger (214).

However, this state of solitude was broken by his encounter with Bilbo and Frodo. Like Gollum, they too had possessed the Ring. Monda focusses on the relationship between Gollum and Frodo, stating that each of these characters is mirrored in the other. In Frodo, Gollum sees himself as Sméagol once more, while Frodo sees in Gollum his future with the Ring (135-137).

This shows how Tolkien managed to narrate events, describe places, and convey emotions through parallels and foils. Both Frodo and Gollum are the protagonists in the final events of *The Lord of the Rings*. Gollum's actions in the Crack of Doom leads Monda to consider Gollum an *alter Christus*, bringing the two Hobbits even closer together.

For Monda, a Christological image can be glimpsed in the character of Gollum. Like Christ, Gollum carries the sins of the world and, in this way, frees the world of them. Like Christ, Gollum makes the descent '*ad inferos*': he immerses himself in the lava just as Christ immersed himself in the waters of the River Jordan. Therefore, Gollum effectively represents the irony of Christ: that is, that of the cursed one who dies to destroy the Ring (137-139).

For Christ and Gollum, death has a 'sacrificial' and 'redemptive' meaning. Their deaths saved their respective worlds from evil and transformed a curse into a blessing for all.

2.4 Verlyn Flieger: Gollum and Frodo between Fate and Free Will

In *Splintered Light. Logos and Language in Tolkien's World* (2002), Verlyn Flieger focusses on the conflict between Fate and Free Will in the characters of Gollum and Frodo (cf. also Flieger, 1981, 59-60).

She finds in Tolkien's writings a game of moving away from the light for different reasons, as well as continuous interactions between Fate and Free Will. Flieger identifies an existential tension between Frodo and Gollum, in which the Self is mirrored in the Other. Finally, there exists the possibility for the Hobbits to act outside of the Music of the Ainur.

In the last part of *The Lord of the Rings*, Flieger sees the possibility of remedying the failures caused by evil's attraction in both Frodo and Gollum (Flieger, 2002, 215-219).

2.5 Tom Shippey: Gollum and his 'addiction' to the Ring

In *The Road to Middle-earth* (2005), Tom Shippey examined Gollum's 'addiction' to the Ring, comparing the Ring to heroin and Gollum to a drug addict:

> Actually all the doubts just mentioned can be cleared up by the use of one word, though it is a word never used in *The Lord of the Rings*. The Ring is 'addictive'. All readers probably assimilate Gollum early on to the now-familiar image of a 'drug-addict', craving desperately for a 'fix' even though he knows it will kill him. […] What Gandalf said to Frodo at the start, we should realise, was that he might be able to give the Ring away or destroy it, though only with a struggle; he

could not however be made to *want* to do so (except by some kind of dangerous thought-control). In the end Frodo does want to destroy the Ring but has not the strength. Gollum is accordingly necessary after all – a striking irony. Extending the parallel with heroin one may say that addicts can be cured by the use of external force, and often they have to be, though their co-operation certainly helps. To expect them to break their syringes and throw away their drugs by will-power alone, though, is to confuse an addiction, which is physical, with habit, which is moral. In this aspect of the Ring as in others Tolkien is totally consistent. (157-158)

Shippey emphasises the inner anguish that the Ringbearers experience: the physical need and longing for the desired object are characterised in Gollum and taken to extreme consequences.

Certainly, this analysis has the merit of bringing the theme of the influence of the Ring on the various protagonists of *The Hobbit* and *The Lord of the Rings* back to the attention of readers and academics. However, on the other hand, in my opinion, this type of comparison with heroin addiction is not fully convincing. In reality, it runs the risk of oversimplifying the character of Gollum and the true essence of the Ring.

Above all, Shippey's statement that the addiction caused by the Ring is more physical than moral in nature – the letter being the section in which the concept of 'vice' would instead fall – may not fully convey the complexities of the situation (157-158).

For the reasons that I will develop in the course of the next chapters, I will try to show that, in reality, the Ring acted precisely on a 'moral level'. Any physical degradation is merely a consequence of having complied with its wishes.

Therefore, as Tolkien also stated in his letter n. 181, dated January-February 1956, addressed to Michael Straight, Gollum – having an existential relationship with the Ring and having not fixed his will towards good during the debate in the slag hole (Tolkien, 2006c, 234-235) – fell into evil and succumbed to the seductions and temptations of his beloved, and simultaneously hated, 'Precious'.

2.6 Roberto di Scala: Gollum between ups and downs and lights and shadows

In "Gollum tra alti e bassi: luci e ombre del viaggio nel male" (1999), Roberto Di Scala attempted to consolidate conflicting themes in Gollum's journey, such as "up" and "down", "dark" and "light", and "good" and "bad" (1-5).

This dualistic approach led Di Scala to stress the change that took place in *The Lord of the Rings* and the conclusive reconstitution of perfect order in the final scene in the Crack of Doom. In it, he notes an inseparable relationship between the two survivors of the Mount Doom flames: Frodo and Sméagol, with the latter being the "good part of Gollum" and now being one with Frodo, despite not having physically survived (3-4).

Although very suggestive, Di Scala's analysis risks boxing the character of Gollum under the limiting label of *doppelgänger*, creating a strong dichotomy between Gollum and Sméagol and an excessive identification between Sméagol and Frodo.

In the following chapters I will underline the fact that, in the character of Gollum, the inclination to devote himself to evil was already present before finding the Ring. I will try to clarify this point by connecting Tolkien's stories with his letters. Furthermore, I will prove that, at the moment of Gollum's death, it is not possible to clearly trace a precise and unequivocal division in his soul to the point of considering Sméagol completely good and almost revived in Frodo.

2.7 Gollum and other characters of world literature

Over time, there have been many analyses of the figure of Gollum in relation to other characters of world literature. By way of example, briefly and concisely, only three parallelisms will be mentioned in these pages, in which Gollum has been compared to the characters of two works by Shakespeare and to one of the protagonists of a novel by Dostoevsky. The common thread in these analyses is the idea of the 'double' present both in the character of Sméagol-Gollum and in those narrated by the other authors mentioned.

2.7.1 Lisa Hopkins: Gollum and Caliban

Especially regarding the characterisation of the figure of Gollum, one of the writers closest to Tolkien is undoubtedly Shakespeare. Actually, in 2007 a book entitled *Tolkien and Shakespeare: Essays on Shared Themes and Language,* edited by J. Brennan Croft, was published. In it, in the part entitled "The Other", there are two essays that deal with Gollum in relation to two Shakespearean characters: Caliban and Othello.

In this section, I will analyse the first of the aforementioned essays, written by Lisa Hopkins: "Gollum and Caliban. Evolution and Design" (Hopkins, 2007, 281-293). In it, the author compared Tolkien's stories with the text of Shakespeare's play *The Tempest*, which saw its first staging in the early Seventeenth Century.

It is known that Tolkien had a conflicting relationship with Shakespeare. In fact, in letter n. 151 of 18th September 1954 addressed to Hug Brogan, he wrote:

> Also I now deeply regret having used Elves, though this is a word in ancestry and original meaning suitable enough. But the disastrous debasement of this word, in which Shakespeare played an unforgiveable pan, has really overloaded it with regrettable tones, which are too much to overcome. (Tolkien, 2006c, 185)

Or in a note of the letter n. 163 of 7th June 1955 written to W.H. Auden, speaking about the Ents, he wrote:

> Their part in the story is due, I think, to my bitter disappointment and disgust from schooldays with the shabby use made in Shakespeare of the coming of 'Great Birnam wood to high Dunsinane hill': I longed to devise a setting in which the trees might really march to war. (Tolkien, 2006c, 212)

However, this shows that Tolkien knew Shakespeare's works and, when he could, he also went to see them at the theatre (cf. 88). As regards *The Tempest*, it is interesting to read the letter n. 64 of 30th April 1944 intended for his son Christopher, in which he demonstrated that he had read this Shakespearean text, stating that: "On the whole Sam is behaving well, and living up to repute. He treats Gollum rather like Ariel to

Caliban" (77). This reference could simply mean that Tolkien had modelled the relationship between Sam and Gollum after that of Ariel and Caliban.

However, Lisa Hopkins has argued that there is a deeper correspondence between the two 'monstrous' creatures. The author stated about Gollum and Caliban: they loved shiny things; they were isolated and alien to the linguistic context of those around them (i.e. they did not speak in the same way as their contemporaries); they had planned to betray their master while he slept; both were associated with fish and were seen as expert but unreliable guides on a journey to an unknown place; and finally, both had claimed ownership of something as their own (Hopkins, 2007, 283).

Despite all this, the author underlined that the greatest point of comparison between Gollum and Caliban is to be found in the relationship between the couples Gollum-Frodo and Prospero-Caliban. Actually, in both cases, each had recognised himself in the other. In the case of Frodo and Gollum, then, there was not only a literal relationship – in fact, Gollum was a descendant of the Hobbits – but there was a much larger established pattern. In reality, the fates of both were closely connected and the similarities between the two were greater than the differences (284).

2.7.2 Charles Keim: Gollum and Othello

The second text it is necessary to consider, contained in the collective book concerning the relationship between Tolkien and Shakespeare, is the essay written by Charles Keim, entitled: "Of Two Minds. Gollum and Othello" (2007, 294-312). In my analysis, I will limit myself to reflecting only on some of the essential points of this article.

First of all, for the author, Gollum and Othello are two characters who are internally divided but in different ways. Othello is considered the exemplification of the internal struggle between good and evil ('psychomachia') present in him but externalised through the figures of Iago ('the bad angel') and Desdemona ('the good angel'). However, the real dissociation arose in him only after he has strangled and murdered Desdemona. In that moment, he decided to draw distance from himself.

In the story of Gollum, another strangulation, committed by Sméagol against Déagol, led to a much longer inner degradation, caused by the guilt of that atrocious act which led to profound consequences. Gollum became divided and his identity was contested between two voices fighting against each other. At the same time, any kind of 'umpire', with the power to decide which thought to listen to, was absent in him.

As Keim masterfully stated, Gollum was not a schizophrenic. In fact, each part of his divided consciousness knew of the existence of the other. Neither part is totally good and, for this reason, it is not possible to affirm that the internal feud between Sméagol and Gollum was a representation of the struggle between good and evil.

Therefore, the complexity of this character cannot be hastily dismissed as being representative of a 'schizophrenic Manichaeism' or a 'Manichean bipolarism': it would not restore truth to this magnificent and unfortunate creature (295-96). Indeed, Keim described the relationship between Sméagol and Gollum as thus:

> At this point, we verge on committing the error of interpreting Gollum and Sméagol as two sides of a single character rather than separate personalities within a single body; but we still cannot be certain that it is Gollum who is full of wickedness and Sméagol who can be trusted. Sméagol is not the unfallen Gollum, nor does he represent an innate sense of goodness. He is a desperate as Gollum to retrieve the Ring. It was Sméagol, after all, who first murdered Déagol for it. (304)

The certainties that have always characterised the interpretation of this character hypothetically divided between 'bad Gollum' and 'good Sméagol', should be set aside to make room for a more realistic vision of things.

Indeed, Sméagol killed Déagol. They both wanted the Ring and would do almost anything to get it. In the next chapters, I will better specify why the term 'almost' has been used in my previous statement. In fact, the nuances that Tolkien inserted in his story do not allow the reader to be clear-cut or rigid in their judgments and analyses of the characters of Middle-earth.

Furthermore, in his essay, speaking of the fall of Othello and comparing it to that of Gollum, Keim showed that the deaths of these two characters turn out to be very different. In fact, at the end of their lives, both had managed to kiss and hold their 'treasures' in their hands: Desdemona on one side and the Ring on the other. However, Othello died by his own hand as a final act of contrition in an ultimate act of love. Instead, Gollum, by falling into the lava, had been "brought to justice", along with all his inner torments and unresolved problems (308-311).

This ending has a much deeper meaning than it may appear at first. Actually, the justice to which Gollum had been delivered was at the same time Eternal Love, Divine Providence and Infinite Mercy.

2.7.3 Stefano Giorgianni: Gollum in a confrontation with Dostoevsky

The third, and last, comparison between Gollum and other characters in world literature, is taken from an essay published in 2015, in a volume entitled *Tolkien e i classici*. This article was written by Stefano Giorgianni and is entitled: "Il doppio tra Tolkien e Dostoevskij. Viaggio nella parte oscura della natura umana" (2015, 163-168).

After reviewing the points of contact between Tolkien and Dostoevsky, the author thus affirmed that both writers managed to narratively render both the greatness of Man and his centrality in creation, and the different tensions present in the human soul which can also lead to a moral and existential degradation caused by a fascination with evil. The latter, if not well controlled and destroyed at its root, can cause men and women to get lost in the ambivalence of their own soul, remaining in profound darkness (165).

It is precisely in this context that the author spoke about Gollum, continuously placing him in connection with the works of the Russian writer. He pointed out how it is possible to trace such a parallel between Gollum and Golyadkin. Within this comparison, Giorgianni forcefully affirmed the presence of the double essence of these two literary characters: they were divided between their malignant and benign parts, between attraction towards God or Satan and, for this reason, they had shattered their personalities. But, according to the author, they had also managed to unify their own interiority through a titanic effort, with much suffering and sacrifice (165-168).

However, in my opinion, this Manichean and bipolar vision of Gollum does not allow the reader to fully see the truth about the essence of this magnificent character: as I will try to explain in the following chapters, Gollum was not a 'double', nor did he voluntarily choose to throw himself into the fires of Mount Doom. Indeed, using Gandalf's words, it could be said that, behind the events at the Crack of Doom, there was 'another power at work'.

2.8 Lucia Opreanu: Gollum between identity and dualism

A further analysis about the character of Gollum was developed by Lucia Opreanu in an article published in 2011 in the *Journal of the University of Bucharest*, entitled: "The inescapable other-identity transitions and mutations in the construction of Tolkien's Gollum/Sméagol" (151-159).

The author started from a general consideration according to which, in Tolkien's writings, identities are built through, and not outside, differences, and that the relationship with the other is crucial for the definition of one's being. In this context, in reference to the character of Gollum, she underlined:

> In his case the natural process of identity formation seems to be reversed as combined influence of the Ring, the nether world of darkness and water he chooses to inhabit and his own innate character make him undergo a process of physical and moral devolution. (153)

Therefore, for the author, Gollum's identity can be traced through the analysis of his moral, social or existential dimensions, connected to the influence that the Ring had in his life. Starting from this assumption, she added that Gollum cannot be interpreted simply as an 'anti-Frodo', as a parody of another protagonist of Middle-earth stories for the sole purpose of building the figure of the brave hero. According to Opreanu, in line with the theory of the 'double' ("*doppelgänger*"), one should identify the similarities and differences between Gollum and Frodo, their way of relating to each other, and the internal relationship which exists between Gollum and Sméagol (154).

Precisely in reference to this last point, the author has highlighted how, in *The Hobbit*, Gollum used the term 'precious' when referring to himself and only later did he also attribute it to the Ring. Furthermore, she noted that the name 'Sméagol' probably derived from the Anglo-Saxon verb 'sméagan' which means to 'scrutinise', 'investigate', 'penetrate', or 'examine', whose adjectival form 'sméah' means 'shrewd', 'acute', 'crafty', or 'subtle' (155).

Continuing the analysis of the names, Opreanu focussed on the terms 'Slinker and Stinker' which Sam used for Gollum and Sméagol. She underlined how, instead, Frodo called Gollum by his Hobbit name, i.e. Sméagol, and urged him to abandon the name Gollum which had been imposed on him by others.

However, Opreanu also highlighted the risks of an analysis of Gollum excessively linked to the 'double' theory, stating that:

> A potential risk of applying the 'doppelgänger' concept to this challenging protagonist concerns the temptation to use the simple binary model suggested by Stevenson's Jekyll/Hyde. […]. Gollum and Sméagol are not only aware of one another but are almost constantly engaged in conversation. In the case of one of their most representative dialogues they are presented as two opposed lines of thought competing at the level of a single mind, two creatures trapped in a single body. (156)

From these statements, a reflection follows about how the risk of perceiving Gollum and Sméagol as two opposite characters and repellent poles has often led to a trivialisation of this extraordinary character's essence. In fact, it is precisely within the internal dialectic of his soul, in the continuous confrontation with himself, that Gollum tried to build his own identity. But, he was already marked by a character which was in itself mischievous and aggravated by the presence of the Ring in his life.

However, Gollum failed to find a solution and a synthesis to these internal, divergent drives of his soul. It has led commentators to put forward interpretations which view this character as an allegory: on the one hand, of the medieval dichotomy of 'soul-body'; or, of the struggle between 'good-evil'; or, finally, mental disorders such as 'schizophrenia' and 'bipolarity' (158).

But, as I will show in the next chapters, Gollum was much more than all this: he cannot be caged by stereotypes framing him as an allegory or a madman with a double personality.

2.9 Yvette Kisor: Gollum and his exile

The last writing it is necessary to refer to in the investigation of Gollum is the one published in 2014 in a collection of essays in honour of Tom Shippey. It was written by Yvette Kisor and titled: "'Poor Sméagol': Gollum as Exile in *The Lord of the Rings*" (153-168).

In this article, the author focussed on the concepts of the 'exiled' man and shown how Tolkien's works were imbued with a 'sense of exile', especially in the attitudes of Elves and Men. According to Kisor, all this emerged from the Professor's Catholic faith, from the mutual belief that there is a Lost Paradise, and that human beings are distanced from God and bliss. She described the figure of Gollum, within this framework of exile, as such:

> But what of Gollum? Tolkien never specifically calls him an exile [...]. In his influential article on the language of exile in Old English poetry, Stanley Greenfield discusses four aspects of the exile state that find expression in the poetic formulae: the status of the exile, the exile's state of mind, movement within or into exile, and the expression of deprivation. Each of these can be applied to Gollum in illuminating ways, and a consideration reveals how for Gollum his Ring, his Precious, takes the place of king or homeland in the *comitatus* relationship. (154)

Therefore, according to the author, it is possible to trace all the four elements of exile in Gollum: that is, the state of exile, the mental condition of an exile, going into exile, and the expression of deprivation. However, all this was mixed in him both with the importance that the Ring had in his life (his Precious, which was jealously guarded) and with his way of speaking in the first and third person, which separated him from the world, from others and from himself.

In her text, Kisor pointed out that, certainly in Gollum, there are echoes of the story of Cain, who killed his brother Abel, while Sméagol murdered his cousin Déagol.

For the author, another possible parallelism exists with the biblical Adam who, having sinned by eating fruit from the Tree of the Knowledge of Good and Evil, was punished and expelled from the Garden of Eden. So too, Gollum was driven out of his village as punishment, having to take refuge in the dark caves of the Misty Mountains.

Furthermore, as in both the English poetic tradition and the story of Gollum, the condition of the exile has been compared to being 'miserable' and 'wretched' (155-157).

However, according to Kisor, there is a specific characteristic of Gollum's character: he did not complain about the distance from his homeland and his loved ones. The only pain that always made him feel 'poor' ('Poor Sméagol') came from fact that he had lost his Ring, his 'Preciousss'.

So, in Gollum's life, this precious object, this evil amulet, replaced all of his past. Only with it did he really feel 'at home'. His true exile was not derived from being expelled from his native country but from the loss of his true Precious: The Ring of Sauron (157-158).

But, as Kisor shrewdly stated, there is a moment within Tolkien's story in which the memory of Sméagol's past resurfaces, forcefully making itself felt and relocating exile into its classic context of distance from home and loved ones.

That moment is Gollum's 'almost conversion' while Frodo and Sam are sleeping at the stairs of Cirith Ungol (158).

Furthermore, in the use of pronouns – in the first or third person – Kisor has precisely identified one of the fundamental themes for understanding the particularity of both the character of Gollum and the essence of his exile, his loss, his detachment from the surrounding world and, often, even by himself.

For Kisor, in the character of Gollum, the concept of exile is not so much connected to the Anglo-Saxon poetic tradition as, rather, to the modern conception of mental and existential alienation:

> His lack of felt connection with any being or place is reflected in Gollum's unconventional pronoun use just as his obsession with the Ring has infiltrated other aspects of his referential language – his Precious is sometimes the Ring and sometimes himself, and it is often nearly impossible to determine which Gollum intends as the conflation between the two is all but complete. (163)

For the author, all this shows that Tolkien was a man who loved the Medieval Age and was rooted in it but, at the same time, an attentive expert of the present, a writer perfectly inserted into the Twentieth Century.

3. Voices in the Darkness: Gollum between Cinema and Dubbing

In analysing the character of Gollum, it is impossible not to refer, albeit briefly, to how he has been represented cinematically (see also Casagrande, 2022, 70-88). At the beginning of the

2000s, the New Zealand director Peter Jackson made him well-known to a wide general world public, first within the movie trilogy of *The Lord of the Rings* (Shippey, 2004, 233-254) and then in his adaptation of *The Hobbit*. The success of the films worldwide was also greatly aided by the various adaptations into foreign languages, thanks to quality dubbing. An emblematic case is the Italian version.

Therefore, in this next section, the character of Gollum will be examined through the stories of those who 'gave him a voice', but in a hidden way: through a book reading, or the new technologies of cinematographic art, or in a dark dubbing room. It can rightly be said that he is well-known to viewers thanks to many 'voices in the darkness'.

3.1 Characteristics of the 'voice of Gollum'

Before addressing the topic of those who have 'given a voice' to this character, it is interesting to ascertain what the essential characteristics of his vocality are. According to Woody and Susan Wendling:

> Gollum's speech has two distinctive qualities. First in the snake-like sibilant "s" [...]. The sibilant "s" is reminiscent of the serpent in the Garden of Eden (Genesis 3). The second distinctive quality is the sound of being strangled: [...] Sméagol had strangled his brother Deagol to possess the ring, reminiscent of Cain who slew his brother Abel (Genesis 4). (Wendling, 2012, 2)

So the first of Gollum's two vocal characteristics was the sibilant *s* (which, according to the authors, referred to the tempting serpent from the third chapter of the Book of Genesis). Indicative of this characteristic are two annotations that Tolkien made in two different texts. In point, there is this example in the fifth chapter of *The Hobbit*: "Suddenly up came Gollum and whispered and hissed" (Tolkien, 2011, 68). As another example, there is this commentary on the Puffin edition of *The Hobbit*, in the letter n. 236 dated 30th December 1961 addressed to Rayner Unwin, where he stated as follows:

> I believe there is only one error remaining in the text from which the Puffin was printed: *like* for *likes* […]. This crept in in the 6th imp. I think. Not that Gollum would miss the chance of a sibilant! (2006c, 313)

The second characteristic is Gollum's choked voice, which the authors have linked to the fact that Sméagol choked Déagol just as Cain killed Abel in the story in the fourth chapter of Genesis.

These elements are fundamental to understanding what kind of voice Gollum has been given both in cinema and on radio.

3.2 J.R.R. Tolkien: Gollum as read by his creator

Almost unexpectedly, the first to have 'given a voice' to Gollum was Tolkien himself. In fact, in August 1952 the Professor, who went to see his friend George Sayer in Malvern, recorded a tape containing part of Chapter V of *The Hobbit*. This recording was later released under the title: *J.R.R. Tolkien Reads and Sings His "The Hobbit" and "The Fellowship of the Ring"* (see Tolkien, 2017a, 132).

This episode is referred to by Tolkien himself in the letter n. 134 of 29th August 1952 addressed to Rayner Unwin:

> I have recently made some tape-recordings of parts of the Hobbit and The Lord (notably the Gollum-passages and some pieces of 'Elvish') and was much surprised to discover their effectiveness as recitations, and (if I may say so) my own effectiveness as a narrator, I do a very pretty Gollum and Treebeard. (Tolkien, 2006c, 164)

Therefore, the first 'voice given' to Gollum was that of his own creator: from Tolkien's mind, it was first imprinted in ink through the tales of his Secondary World and then resurfaced in the Primary World through his own warm voice.

Gollum and Tolkien met that summer in the early 1950s: author and character, sub-creator and creature, finally reunited in a whisper.

3.3 Andy Serkis: Gollum in the Cinema

In Peter Jackson's two film trilogies, the characters of Sméagol and Gollum were played by British actor Andy Serkis. Through modern technology and special effects, he managed to provide, in a masterly way, movements and vocal nuances that enriched and embellished this extraordinary character. Furthermore, the actor also represented Sméagol in the duel with Déagol for ownership of the Ring.

In 2003, Serkis wrote and published a book titled: *Gollum: How We Made Movie Magic*. In it, he retraced and recounted his adventures as Gollum in *The Lord of the Rings* trilogy. Regarding the construction and recreation of Gollum's voice, the actor said:

> I started to think about where [Gollum] would physically carry his pain, and decided that his throat could be deeply affected, constricted by subconscious guilt associated with killing Deagol, so that when he talked he felt like he was choking. (4)

So, to better embody Gollum's voice, Serkis looked to Sméagol's guilt over Déagol's murder. Thus Gollum's throat, indelibly marked by that terrible and merciless event, could only emit the same last strangled sound that emerged from the mouth of his dying cousin. Furthermore, the actor explained that, for Gollum's voice, he also referred to the behaviour and sounds emitted by a cat choking on a fur ball.

3.4 Francesco Vairano: Gollum and the art of Dubbing in Italy

In Italy, Peter Jackson's films have become famous and well-known to the general public (Cilli, 2016, 263-276) with help from the extraordinary dubbing work entrusted to Francesco Vairano. He was Voice Actor, Dialogist and Director of Dubbing for both of the Middle-earth trilogies (*The Lord of the Rings* and *The Hobbit*), along with the TV series *The Lord of the Rings – The Rings of Power* and the *Harry Potter* film saga. In the latter, Vairano provided the voice for Professor Severus Snape, played masterfully by Alan Rickman.

The art of dubbing did, and still does, carry great prestige in Italy. Therefore, it is necessary to particularly reflect on how much Gollum has entered the collective imagination of Italian viewers and readers, thanks to these cinematographic works.

Actually, in many cases, especially among young people

born or raised in the 2000s, watching Peter Jackson's films preceded reading Tolkien's books. For this reason, especially in Italy, the figure of Gollum – as well as that of the other characters – is inextricably linked to the somatic features and the voice with which he has been characterised in the films.

During various interviews, which are available on the internet, conducted between 2011 and 2017, Francesco Vairano spoke about the extraordinary experience he had during those years working on Jackson's films. Through these, he has provided a window for the path that led him to 'build' the voice of such a particular and complex creature as Sméagol/Gollum.

Vairano underlined how interesting and stimulating it was to play the character because, according to him:

> It rarely happens in an actor's life playing a character with multiple faces: usually either all good or all bad. Instead, Gollum was sometimes good, sometimes bad, sometimes half and half; you never understood – a fascinating challenge for an actor. (Arsenale Cinema, 2015; min. 6:48-7:11)

Furthermore, he noted that he

> [...] related to Snape and Gollum for a reason: they are extremely interesting characters for an actor because they are not one-faceted, and that's it, but they have multiple sides. There is the 'double' and there is nothing more challenging for an actor than to play a character who's sometimes good, sometimes bad, you don't know how he's going to act. It's a stimulus and a challenge for an actor. (Lucca Comics & Games, 2017; min. 10:45-11:29)

This difficulty, mixed with a sense of fascination, led Vairano to reflect on the type of technical and existential preparation that the figure and voice of Gollum needed. He thus stated:

> To make a character like Gollum, you need an experience of your own or of someone else you've met: there is desperation, the impossibility of having things, the wear-out of something that you desperately want. All of these are things that a young actor can't reproduce, whereas for a more mature actor it's easier. (Arsenale Cinema, 2015; min. 10:30-11:01)

Or, again:

> You must be more mature not only in terms of age but also from the life you have led, the people you have met. Because Gollum is all magma, there is a perennial dualism in him. (Enciclopedia del Doppiaggio, 2011; min. 36:16-36:33)

And, finally:

> In Gollum, an actor and dubber must put into the character all the pain, passion, despair, nostalgia, longing for, and interpret a 'creature', because Gollum has become a creature from the very normal Hobbit he was. The Ring has complicated his existence. (Lucca Comics & Games, 2017; min. 11:30-11:58)

It is precisely this tormented experience and perennial dualism which had to also be reflected through the character's voice. In order to enhance the character, there was a need for an exceptional vocal quick-change artist like Francesco Vairano who, in the same way that Andy Serkis did in the original English adaptation, had to combine different types of registers:

that of a deep and hoarse voice, for Gollum, and of a thin, high-pitched voice, for Sméagol.

A further problem arose with the adaptation of the dialogue from English to Italian. More precisely, a problem existed with respect to Gollum's sibilant *s*. In the original English, the expression 'my Preciousss' is easy to render vocally, as it is enough to prolong the *s* at the end of the word to create the snakelike effect desired by Tolkien. In Italian, though, all this was more complicated to achieve as the 's' is contained within, rather than at the end of, the equivalent word, 'Tesoro' (Treasure).

This led Vairano to reflect on whether it was more appropriate to keep the term 'Tesoro' or if it would be better to replace it with 'Delizia' (Delight), so as to have the snake sound towards the end of the word.

However, following discussion with members of the Società Tolkieniana Italiana, who had helped him to correct the texts and dialogues, it was decided that this change could not be accepted, as it was not possible to ignore the classic Italian translation of *The Lord of the Rings*, in which 'Tesoro' was used for 'Precious' (Arsenale Cinema, 2015; min. 13:57-15.33).

For this reason, Francesco Vairano, seeing his proposal for a terminological change rejected and thinking about how to keep the same 's' sound present in the original English, decided to mark and lengthen this letter within the word.

Thus, necessity, becoming a virtue, fortunately led to one of the most famous expressions used by young Italians at the beginning of the 2000s. It became widely used to communicate affection and love towards another person, with an emphasis worthy of Tolkien and Gollum, to call someone your 'Tesssoro' (Associazione Culturale Sentieri Tolkieniani, 2014; min. 23:35-24:50).

Chapter 2

Gollum And The Hobbit: 'Riddles In The Dark'

Introduction

The long journey undertaken in the previous chapter now allows the reader to delve into the crucial question that motivated and started this book: that is, whether there could be a connection between the character of Gollum and the passage from the Gospel of Luke (also present in the Gospel of Matthew), in which Jesus said: "For where your treasure is, there also will your heart be" (Lk 12:34).

Our investigation begins with *The Hobbit* both in its original version and in the modified one after *The Lord of the Rings* began to formulate in Tolkien's mind. Indeed, it is in *The Hobbit*, in this 'round trip' to the 'reconquest of a treasure', lost and preserved under the evil wings of the ancient dragon Smaug, that Gollum first appeared on the literary scene of Middle-earth. He initially had an important but ancillary function. Subsequently, however, he assumed a fundamental role that made him a genuine protagonist of Tolkien's stories.

The Professor had bet on the Ring and Gollum to the point where he made a gesture which, at first sight, appears to be incredible: changing the nature of an imaginary character from his published work. In fact, in *The Hobbit*, passing from one edition to the other, one finds 'two Gollums', each completely different. Therefore, 'duplicity' marked this character from the beginning: even before affecting the binomial Sméagol/Gollum, it characterised the very essence of the first edition's Gollum differently from that of the second.

At the origin of all this, there was the awareness that the centre of interest of the story had to move from a 'treasure' (the Arkenstone) to another 'Treasure' (the Ring of Power) (Flieger, 2014, 65-77). In the transition between these two treasures, the metamorphosis of a 'third treasure' is also included: the famous 'Preciousss' of Gollum.

1. *The Hobbit*: A Children's Tale?

These pages will not address all the themes contained in *The Hobbit* nor will I focus on the synthesis of its plot, which is now known worldwide. Rather, it is necessary to explore two themes that are at the heart of the story: the reason why this text was written and the message it carries.

In this context, one must also ask to whom Tolkien's works on Middle-earth were directed. They have often been defined as 'works for children' or 'stories for teenagers'. However, I cannot share this opinion. In fact, if the relationship between 'fairy-tales' and 'children' in *The Hobbit* is analysed, it can be noted that: surely the first and most urgent motivation that prompted the Professor to write this book was to tell fairy-tales to his children. This did not prevent him from including some themes in the story that were anything but for children, though (Tolkien, 2017a, 89, note 17).

The Professor dedicated a long paragraph in his essay "On Fairy-stories" (Tolkien, 2006b, 49-65), to this issue and also in the draft letter n. 215 of April 1959, in which he answered some questions from Walter Allen about the publisher's request to contribute to a symposium to be published in the *New Statesman*'s children's book supplement (Tolkien, 2006c, 296-299).

From these texts, it is clear that Tolkien was against the conventions established by an editorial system which imposed hackneyed clichés, including the one whereby fairy-tales were considered a narrative literary genre purely for children. Here, then, is the essential question: who are children? For Tolkien, they were not a social class to be provided with preconceived literary food. Instead, he saw them as people in training, at a different degree of maturity to adults. In fact, some children, and teenagers, possess a decidedly greater maturity than that of adults.

Tolkien knew this well and appreciated it because he believed so much in children and in their capacity for human, intellectual and linguistic maturation, so much so that he also proposed stories for them that were not merely for children but a 'literature that is above our measure'. To do this, he wrote stories capable of overcoming many pre-established ideological barriers and did not claim to state *a priori* what was suitable for a child and what was not.

For this reason, readers of the Professor's works can never be measured by parameters that are valid for everyone in every place and time. On the contrary, the public must measure themselves with their own abilities, going beyond their own measure, adopting a new language and experiencing a totally fantastic literary, and human, adventure.

2. The heart of *The Hobbit* and 'the Gospel of Gollum'

Taking all this into account, it is necessary to deepen the internal themes of *The Hobbit*. Reading this work, one realises that, in it, there is a triptych of concepts united together. Tolkien managed to keep together, alternately and variously described:

a) The treasure;
b) The theft (or being a thief);
c) The murder (or death in general).

There are many examples which could be provided but I will limit myself to mentioning only a few. For instance, as regards Bilbo, he was hired by Gandalf and the Dwarves as a burglar (theft) in order to penetrate the depths of Erebor, and steal the Arkenstone (treasure) from the dragon Smaug, even at the risk of his life (death).

Furthermore, even the story involving Smaug as the focal character had been marked by the desire for a treasure, which was resolved with the death of the Dwarves and the theft of all their gold.

Even the return of the Dwarves to Erebor repeats the same triptych: Smaug, having stolen the treasure from the Dwarves, deserved their hatred and desire for revenge, culminating in his death and the reconstitution of the old Kingdom under the Mountain.

Additionally, the meeting between Bilbo and Gollum is also characterised by the presence of a treasure (the Ring), which is voluntarily or involuntarily stolen by Bilbo (who was considered for a long time, a thief), which caused Gollum's desperation and desire for revenge, and was also willing to kill Mr Baggins just to get it back (murder).

Finally, if you think about it, even the clash between Sméagol and Déagol, as recounted in *The Lord of the Rings*, reproposed this triptych: Sméagol, desiring the ring Déagol found, killed him and seized possession by stealing it from him (Christie, 2013, 83-101).

Therefore, it is evident how wealth, the immoderate lust for treasures, gold and precious objects, and the tragic consequences of this perverse desire, are central themes of both *The Hobbit* and what I call 'the Gospel of Gollum'.

First of all, it must be remembered that *The Hobbit* was not born as a preparatory story for *The Lord of the Rings*. Tolkien admitted as much in letter n. 23 of 17th February 1938 intended for C.A. Furth: "The Hobbit sequel is still where it was, and I have only the vaguest notions of how to proceed. Not ever intending any sequel, I fear I squandered all my favourite 'motifs' and characters on the original 'Hobbit'" (Tolkien, 2006c, 29). Or again, in letter n. 24 of the following day addressed to Stanley Unwin, he wrote: "I squandered so much on the original 'Hobbit' (which was not meant to have a sequel) that it is difficult to find anything new in that world" (29).

Therefore, the 'original Hobbit' (the first version) had a completely different structure and meaning compared to the later *The Hobbit*, which acted as a prequel to *The Lord of the Rings*. This is of fundamental importance, as it allows the reader to fully understand the profound meaning of this text and how its meaning was subsequently channelled as a tributary of the stories told in Tolkien's masterpiece of the Ring.

Therefore, if the first edition of *The Hobbit* is considered, I cannot fail to agree with Andrea Monda, according to whom the whole story of that book would exemplify the evangelical passage (cf. Monda, 2013):

> Do not store up for yourselves treasures on earth, where moth and decay destroy, and thieves break in and steal. But store up treasures in heaven, where neither moth nor decay destroys, nor thieves break in and steal. For where your treasure is, there also will your heart be. (Matt 6:19-21)

All of the content above preceding the last sentence can be glimpsed in two particular and clearly identifiable passages of this first Tolkien story set in the Third Age of Middle-earth. The first of these scenes, which clearly shows this characteristic, sees Bilbo as the protagonist. When speaking with the Bard and the King of the Elves, in the act of giving them the Arkenstone, which he had stolen from Smaug and had hidden from the Dwarves, he stated:

> "You may see it!" said he. "It is this!" and he drew forth the Arkenstone, and threw away the wrapping. The Elvenking himself, whose eyes were used to things of wonder and beauty, stood up in amazement. Even Bard gazed marveling at it in silence. It was as if a globe had been filled with moonlight and hung before them in a net woven of the glint of frosty stars. "This is the Arkenstone of Thrain," said Bilbo, "the Heart of the Mountain; and it is also the heart of Thorin. He values it above a river of gold." (Tolkien, 2011, 248)

While in the eighteenth chapter, entitled 'The Return Journey', after narrating Thorin's death, Tolkien recounted the ending of the story thus:

Actually it was some days before Bilbo really set out. They buried Thorin deep beneath the Mountain, and Bard laid the Arkenstone upon his breast. 'There let it lie till the Mountain falls' he said. 'May it bring good fortune to all his folk that dwell here after!' (Tolkien, 2011, 265)

These two texts allow the reader to understand how close the connection was in the author's mind between 'treasure' and the 'heart' of a person; in this case in relation to Thorin, but also to Bilbo himself. Through the different attitudes of these two characters regarding the Arkenstone, the reader can actually understand that Jesus' sentence, "For where your treasure is, there also will your heart be" can actually represent the general principle exemplified in *The Hobbit*.

As for Thorin, he was insanely chained to this precious gem. Indeed, he felt the full weight of a Dwarf's propensity for treasure. This was compounded by the evil influence Smaug had shed upon that gold all those years and by a boundless lust for the Arkenstone. This visceral relationship between the 'King of the Dwarves' and the 'Heart of the Mountain' is strongly expressed in Bilbo's phrase, according to which the Arkenstone is the 'heart of Thorin', and also by the Bard's gesture of placing this most precious gem on the chest of the dead King.

However, there is a substantial difference between these events. In the first case, the treasure had literally intoxicated Thorin's heart: the desire for the Arkenstone was holding the King in its mortal coil. In the second case, he had not looked for that precious stone but it had come to him from the Bard's hands, delicately placed on the chest of the dead King, no longer an object to be coveted but a sign of luck and prosperity to admire. This had happened because, before expiring, Thorin had asked Bilbo for forgiveness for his actions and words, thus regaining his tranquillity, his friendship with the Hobbit, and his desire to be free and no longer a slave (262-263).

Furthermore, wanting to underline the difference in attitude between Hobbits and Dwarves, Tolkien stressed the fact that Bilbo had not let himself be subjugated by the spell of treasures and gold. This may also be the explanation for why, in *The Lord of the Rings*, Bilbo managed to make the 'great refusal' that no one else had ever dared to make: to leave the Ring and entrust it to Frodo.

Bilbo had been able to do this because, in *The Hobbit*, he had already found himself in that same situation when, voluntarily, he had handed the Arkenstone to Bard and the Elvenking. Certainly, the attraction of such a precious stone had played a decisive role for him too, but he had not succumbed to that temptation, since his heart was not with the treasure but rather in his friendship with Thorin. This had allowed him to earn not only honour and wealth, to which he was not at all attached, but the salvation of his friend and a return home to his beloved shire.

3. The 'first' and 'second' Gollum in *The Hobbit*

Gollum first appeared in Middle-earth in the fifth chapter of *The Hobbit*, entitled 'Riddles in the Dark'. The story of how Bilbo met this monster living in the depths of the caves is now known to all fans of the Professor's stories. However, it is essential to carry out an in-depth analysis of this chapter to try to further understand what Tolkien wanted to communicate through the bizarre encounter between two fascinating creatures and central characters of his Secondary World.

3.1 Gollum in the first edition of The Hobbit

On his way to Erebor, Bilbo found himself in a cave under the Misty Mountains. There, he met Gollum and engaged in a riddle contest with him. This linguistic dispute had something at stake. The precise point of the narrative was the one most subject to modifications by Tolkien when he decided to prepare *The Hobbit* as a prequel to *The Lord of the Rings*.

In fact, in the current version, the rules of engagement of this competition are described by Gollum in this way:

> It must have a competition with us, my preciouss! If precious asks, and it doesn't answer, we eats it, my preciousss. If it asks us, and we doesn't answer, then we does what it wants, eh? We shows it the way out, yes! (Tolkien, 2011, 70)

In the original 1937 version, however, the final part of this statement involved the delivery of a gift by Gollum to Bilbo (Tolkien, 2017a, 136, note 12).

The differences between the first and second editions of *The Hobbit* have been well highlighted and summarised in an acute and pioneering work by Bonniejean Christensen in her 1975 article (republished in 2003) entitled: "Gollum's Character Transformation in *The Hobbit*" (Christensen, 2003, 7-26).

In this essay, the author placed the original text of this chapter and the subsequently modified one in a synoptic way, in order to show the differences between them. According to the author:

> In *The Hobbit* [Gollum] is one of a series of fallen creatures on a rising scale of terror. In *The Lord of the Rings* he is an example of the damned individual […] 'Riddles in the Dark', the fifth chapter of *The Hobbit*, is critical. In the first edition Gollum is a lost soul who would kill but who would not violate his oath [...]. In the second hardback edition, [...] Gollum is a withered, totally depraved creature dominated by an evil Ring and capable of any crime. […] In the original version Gollum may be a benighted creature, condemned to separation from his kind, but he is not totally depraved. The two most heinous crimes to Old Norse morality were murder and oath-breaking. Gollum may be guilty of the former but not of the latter. (Christensen, 2003, 7-10)

Therefore, from this analysis it is possible to notice a very different image of Gollum in the first edition of 1937 compared to the one that can be read today in the version known to readers. Pulling the threads of the speech a little, it can be said that initially Gollum was a solitary creature, reminiscent of other mysterious figures living in the caves and mountains in English literature (especially for children). Curiosity prompted him to meet a strange character who was neither a fish nor an orc but a Hobbit, Bilbo Baggins.

Their common passion for riddles resulted in a contest which had as stakes either Bilbo's life, should he lose, or Gollum's gift of a ring which, compared to the current version, was a real birthday gift. Therefore, in this first edition, Gollum had not committed murder in order to get possession of the ring. The latter was a very common object, probably inspired by the tradition of magical gold rings such as that of Gyges told in *The Republic* by Plato, and had only the power to make anyone who wore it invisible.

Gollum's attachment to that ring was not as strong as it is in the second edition. In fact, he himself offered it to Bilbo as a pledge in case of his defeat in the guessing contest. In this first version, it can be noted that Gollum's desperation was caused not so much by the loss of the ring as the impossibility of keeping his word and the oath he made to Bilbo.

In fact, in the original text, he certainly had a strong drive and desire to feed on Bilbo, but at the same time, his intentions were tempered or even dominated by a 'moral correctness' which, given the developments of the second edition, are puzzling. Gollum's desire to 'not cheat' had prevailed over his evil will to kill.

On this point, Christensen's observation is very interesting, according to which, in ancient Norse tradition, the most atrocious crimes were murder (of which Gollum was guilty above all, to get food) and the breaking of a pact or an oath (which Gollum surely could not be accused of). This is evident in the fact that, at Bilbo's request, he had agreed to accompany him on the way out.

This particular last element is a characteristic trait of Tolkien's entire narrative: both in *The Hobbit* and in *The Lord of the Rings*, it is possible to find the story of a character who, not knowing the way, needs a 'guide' to follow. In fact, Gollum had been Bilbo's guide first willingly (in the original edition of *The Hobbit*) and then involuntarily (in the second edition revised by Tolkien). In *The Lord of the Rings*, the Stoor acts as a guide who is 'forced' by Frodo and Sam on the journey to Mordor.

In all these cases, the fact that a person didn't know where to go has led the characters to rely on each other, even when they are enemies.

This dynamic can be also seen in the chapter, 'The White Rider', in *The Two Towers*. In this text, Gandalf is revived and becomes 'The White'. He tells Gimli about his battle with the Balrog in the mines of Moria, and says:

> We fought far under the living earth, where time is not counted. Ever he clutched me, and ever I hewed him, till at last he fled into dark tunnels. […] In that despair my enemy was my only hope, and I pursued him, clutching at his heel. Thus he brought me back at last to the secret ways of Khazad-dûm: too well he knew them all. Ever up now we went, until we came to the Endless Stair. (Tolkien, 2005, 501-502)

In the same way as Gandalf, Bilbo, especially in the second edition of *The Hobbit*, at the bottom of his existential abyss and desperation, decides to follow his enemy, who leads him through places unknown to him towards the path's exit and a freedom that he himself believed lost forever.

3.2 Gollum in the second edition of The Hobbit

To trace the reasons and timing of this change in Gollum's nature, I will consult some letters that Tolkien wrote around the end of the 1940s and the beginning of the 1950s. They show the whole narrative path of the fifth chapter of *The Hobbit*.

In letter n. 109 of 31st July 1947 addressed to his publisher, Sir Stanley Unwin, (Tolkien, 2006c, 121-122), Tolkien was well aware that a link needed to be created between his first story and *The Lord of the Rings*. In fact, the weak point of the story was constituted by the riddle contest between Gollum and Bilbo, and by the fact that the Stoor had promised his ring to Mr. Baggins as a gift.

However, the Professor understood that the Ring could be the unifying element of the two stories. Therefore, the story had to be modified in order to create a narrative continuity. For this reason, having set the Ring as the main object of *The Lord of the Rings*, Gollum could no longer remain a marginal character, as he was in the first edition of *The Hobbit*. The Stoor was to become one of the most important characters of the adventures in Middle-earth.

In fact, in letter n. 111 of 21st September 1947, Tolkien thus wrote to his publisher: "I send [...] some notes on The Hobbit; and [...] a specimen of re-writing of Chapter V of that work" (124).

From this letter, it is revealed that the editing of *The Hobbit* and the writing of *The Lord of the Rings* worked hand-in-hand. Gollum had grown in importance in the story of the Ring and had literally been changed in the editing of the fifth chapter of the first story. From Tolkien's words, it is evident how he was aiming above all to arrange the story concerning Gollum within the second chapter of *The Lord of the Rings*, entitled, 'The Shadow of the Past'. Furthermore, the Professor sent an example to his publisher, as a mere entertainment, not intended for publication, a draft rewrite of 'Riddles in the Dark' for *The Hobbit*.

However, the publisher liked this version so much that it was taken seriously. In fact, as stated in the letter n. 128 of 1st August 1950 (141), he sent Tolkien the proofs of the new edition of *The Hobbit* containing precisely the modified version of the meeting between Bilbo and Gollum in the caves under the Misty Mountains.

This change was approved by Tolkien. The second edition of *The Hobbit* had started, containing the modified fifth chapter. However, it would have caused disorientation for the readers due to the presence of a substantial change both in a part of the text and in the nature of Gollum's character.

For this reason, as reported in the letter n. 129 of 10th September 1950, Tolkien faced several ways ahead of him that he could take, including introducing an explanatory note that would provide the reasons for the change in *The Hobbit* (142).

Tolkien was doubtful about this option and, uncertain about what to do, he chose to remain silent and let the new edition run its course without further investigation. This decision lasted a few days and, on 14th September 1950, in letter n. 130, he wrote to Sir Stanley Unwin: "I have decided to accept the existence of both versions of Chapter Five, so far as the sequel goes" (142).

The note added by Tolkien in the second version of *The Hobbit* explained the changed text of fifth chapter in this way:

> There the true story of the ending of the Riddle Game, as it was eventually revealed (under pressure) by Bilbo to Gandalf, is now given according to the Red Book, in place of the version Bilbo first gave to his friends, and actually set down in his diary. This departure from truth on the part of a most honest hobbit was a portent of great significance. It does not, however, concern the present story, and those who in this edition make their first acquaintance with hobbit-lore need not trouble about it. Its explanation lies in the history of the Ring, as set out in the chronicles of the Red Book of Westmarch, and it must await their publication. (442)

Through this narrative device, the Professor and his editor had put an end to an important problem of internal coherence in the tales of Middle-earth. Thus, *The Lord of the Rings* had an adequate introduction: *The Hobbit*. This text was no longer a story concluded on its own but it had officially become an important part of the great epic story of the Ring and the struggle of the Free Peoples against Sauron, the Dark Lord of Mordor.

3.2.2 Gollum, Bilbo and the Ring of Power

All this has led to fairly important consequences for the characters and objects implicated in the new formulation and narrative of *The Hobbit*. In fact, Gollum, Bilbo and also the Ring of Sauron had suffered radical and sudden changes in their essence. This is explained in a masterful way by Christensen in her article:

> Bilbo is briefly transformed from the grumbling but good-hearted soul of *The Hobbit* into a heroic and compassionate individual. […]. Having stayed his hand, Bilbo has refrained from evil. But he has still to save himself, to turn from the present evil and in the hope of salvation to leap into the dark. […]. Faith: the leap in the dark that a man takes. Bilbo, a hobbit, takes it. [...] Tolkien's chief alterations in 'Riddles in the Dark' change the stakes in the riddle-game, introduce the Ring as a ring of power [...] define the opposing forces in the universe and convert Gollum from a simply lost creature to a totally depraved one. [...] The alterations clearly increase Gollum's role and remove the story from the realm of the nursery tale. (Christensen, 2003, 20-24)

In short, Tolkien has inserted an object into *The Hobbit*, the Ring of Power, possessing an evil nature and its own will, capable of seducing and corrupting the human soul. Therefore, in this story, the protagonists were called to measure themselves against the evil present within and outside of them.

Bilbo, starting off as a simple Hobbit, had become first a spectator of Gollum's inner drama and, then, a heroic figure. He recognised Gollum's misery and, allowed himself to be led by divine grace in a gesture of pity and mercy towards him. According to the author, Bilbo had made a leap into the void, which can also be interpreted as a 'leap of faith'.

As for Gollum, it can be said that Tolkien managed to recreate him entirely, ontologically changing his being. In this second version, the Stoor was one with the Ring, unable to think of himself without it. The 'you' of Gollum, his only company, was that evil object. It became his *alter ego* and he actually called it by the same name which he used for himself: 'My Precioussss'.

In consideration of all this, the evangelical expression, "For where your treasure is, there also will your heart be" (Lk 12:34), through the modification of the fifth chapter of *The Hobbit*, was set in the character of Gollum by Tolkien through an evident exemplification.

For this, the Stoor, while in his first words had invoked a blessing on himself ("Bless us and splash us, my precioussss!") (Tolkien, 2011, 68), in his last cries, corrupted by the desire for Ring, he could desperately only scream curses at Bilbo, towards the thief of his 'Precioussss': "Curse it! curse it! curse it! […] Curse the Baggins! It's gone! What has it got in its pocketses? Oh we guess, we guess, my precious. He's found it, yes he must have. My birthday-present" (79); "Thief, thief, thief! Baggins! We hates it, we hates it, we hates it for ever!" (82).

4. 'Riddles in the Dark': the renewal ethics of Fairy-stories and the solitude of an ignoble prisoner

Taking all this into account, it is essential to delve even deeper into the fifth chapter of *The Hobbit*, starting with its title: 'Riddles in the Dark'.

As I have shown, it tells of a riddle competition whose prize was either the escape route from those dark caves or the life of Mr. Baggins.

However, one wonders if Gollum himself wasn't among those riddles to be solved. That is, whether some of these language games were used by Tolkien to say something more about that 'living enigma' called Gollum.

This interpretation could also explain the *incipit* of the chapter in which the meeting between the Hobbit and the Stoor occurs. At the beginning of the fifth chapter, the caves were 'dark' and Gollum, who is described as "dark as darkness", lived near the "dark water" (Tolkien, 2011, 67-68).

Furthermore, the *incipit* tells the reader what he made, where he lived and his way of speaking and making a guttural sound which caused him to be called 'gollum'. However, it did not tell who or what he was.

In short, Gollum was a real 'mystery to discover', an 'enigma to decipher', a 'story to be told'. In order to do this, Tolkien used the device of riddles. Once again, language games became the tool to enrich the story, to create literature, to give depth to one of his characters. In this manner, Gollum was brought out of the darkness of the caves in which he had holed up and also the dark existential solitude that had gripped him for a long, long time.

4.1 Bilbo Baggins: a "light out of the past" for Gollum

The spark which lit up the darkness of those nooks and crannies beneath the Misty Mountains was the coming of Bilbo Baggins into those cold and dark places. This is explicitly stated by Galdalf in *The Lord of the Rings*, during a dialogue with Frodo at Bag End:

> But there was something else in it, I think, which you don't see yet. Even Gollum was not wholly ruined. He had proved tougher than even one of the Wise would have guessed – as a hobbit might. There was a little corner of his mind that was still his own, and light came through it, as through a chink in the dark: light out of the past. It was actually pleasant, I think, to hear a kindly voice again, bringing up memories of wind, and trees, and sun on the grass, and such forgotten things. (Tolkien, 2005, 54-55)

Therefore, Bilbo's adventure to the Lonely Mountain together with the Dwarves turned into an opportunity for Gollum to find himself, to escape from that physical and existential 'prison' in which he had closed himself and, therefore, to return to life. But, how was all this possible? It was thanks to the memory of a past now forgotten and believed to be almost lost forever.

It should be noted that, in the whole story of Gollum in *The Hobbit* and in *The Lord of the Rings*, memory has a positive and almost moral connotation. It distances itself totally from the loophole that the Elves used to escape from their destiny as immortals in Arda.

In fact, using the terminology of the essay "On Fairy-stories", for Gollum, remembering his past was not a 'Flight of the Deserter' – i.e. a desire to abandon his reality – but was a way to reclaim his name, his history and his own life. In short, the memory resulting from that "light out of the past" can be considered a real 'Escape of the Prisoner'.

4.2 *"Sun on the Daisies": when riddles solve a human mystery*

To try to understand even more deeply how it was possible that simple riddles managed to have an existential meaning for Gollum, it is necessary to quote a sentence from *The Hobbit* – present in both editions – which clarifies why these two characters decided to engage in this tender.

In the fifth chapter, riddles for Gollum

> were all he could think of. Asking them, and sometimes guessing them, had been the only game he had ever played with other funny creatures sitting in their holes in the long, long ago, before he lost all his friends and was driven away, alone, and crept down, down, into the dark under the mountains. (Tolkien, 2011, 69)

Therefore, on the one hand, the game of creating and solving riddles had been proposed by Gollum both to take some time in order to better understand the situation, to investigate who he was facing and what he actually felt; on the other hand, that type of competition reminded him of the moments when he had not yet been so alone and played in the company of his friends. At that time, he had not been wholly absorbed by the darkness of those caverns and nooks beneath the Misty Mountains.

From all this, it is possible to understand the existential weight of those riddles for Gollum. They could have been the lock into which the burglar Bilbo Baggins crept in, becoming the 'light out of the past' that could pierce the darkness in which Gollum had ended up.

Some elements about the formation and conception of the riddles were provided by Tolkien himself in his epistolary. In fact, in letter n. 25 of 1938 addressed to the editor of the *Observer*, it reads as follows:

> And what about the Riddles? There is work to be done here on the sources and analogues. I should not be at all surprised to learn that both the hobbit and Gollum will find their claim to have invented any of them disallowed. (Tolkien 2006c, 32)

Or again in the letter n. 110 of 20th September 1947 addressed to Allen & Unwin, he wrote:

> As for the Riddles: […] I feel also constrained to remark that 'Sun on the Daisies' is not in verse (any more than 'No-legs') being but the etymology of the word 'daisy', expressed in riddle-form. (123)

This last statement about the riddle, whose solution was 'Sun on the Daisies', is fundamental for the purposes of our discussion. In fact, in it are all the elements of the Professor's thought contained in his essay "On Fairy-stories". Actually, he started from a word, 'daisy', whose etymology he wanted to clarify by creating a riddle inserted in a literary context (Tolkien, 2017a, 136-137, notes 16).

So, once again language and literature have merged and illuminated each other. In this philological-literary game it was possible for Gollum to escape the simultaneous existential and physical prisons he found himself in. Indeed, in *The Hobbit*, it reads as follows:

> [Bilbo] was so pleased that he made up one on the spot […]:
> *An eye in a blue face*
> *Saw an eye in a green face.*
> *"That eye is like to this eye"*
> *Said the first eye,*
> *"But in low place*
> *Not in high place."*
> "Ss, ss, ss," said Gollum. He had been underground a long long time, and was forgetting this sort of thing. […] Gollum brought up memories of ages and ages and ages before, when he lived with his grandmother in a hole in a bank by a river, "Sss, sss, my preciousss," he said. "Sun on the daisies it means, it does." (Tolkien, 2011, 70-71)

This is how the Bilbo managed to pierce the darkness of those caves and of Gollum's present existence. The Stoor had begun to relive his memories and to savour the colours, the scents, the warmth of the common life he had lived many years before by the river with his grandmother and his friends. The memory had reactivated parts of his mind and his heart that had been silent for too long. And this is why Gollum, wounded by those images so full of beauty and tenderness, invented a riddle in stark contrast to the one previously stated. He wanted to plunge himself and Bilbo back into the dark prison in which he had holed up so many years before. Indeed, the answer to this new riddle was "Dark" (71).

Therefore, the two characters were plunged back into a dark existence in which the happiness, the life, the light, and the smells were lost. An interesting thing is the fact that, although Gollum was already a murderer in this second edition of *The Hobbit*, a thief, a perjurer, an outcast and ignoble person, he still managed to create poetry, art, and literature through that linguistic game.

This characteristic allows the reader to recover what Tolkien affirmed in the essay "On Fairy-stories" when, quoting a part of the poem "*Mythopoeia*" dedicated to his friend C.S. Lewis, wrote that: the human being, "although now long estranged" and "dis-graced", is not "de-throned" and has "lordship" because he makes "still by the law" in which he is made (Tolkien, 2006b, 144)

Therefore, the Professor's belief was that even a sinful man or a miserable creature like Gollum has the right to sub-create Secondary Worlds made of poems and narratives, through the invention and combination of words, nouns and adjectives. In short, sin or bad morals do not affect the human capacity to create artistic beauty and literary wonder. In fact, even if you were to find yourself in the deepest darkness of your own existence, or in the total darkness of cold solitary caves, poetry could lighten the darkness.

Certainly, what the Fall (as in, original sin) and subsequent falls (the sins which follow) may have affected is the use that human beings can make of this activity in their minds. But, as Tolkien himself said, "*Abusus non tollit usum*" (144). Man is not wholly changed, and though "dis-graced", he has not been "de-throned": he still creates by way of the law in which he has been made. This law is the one, according to the Creator who gave life to all creatures, making them as sub-creators. Gollum also participated in all of this.

However, in front of him, the Stoor had another skilled riddle maker, Bilbo, who this time had asked Gollum an even more important riddle: "A box without hinges, key, or lid, / Yet golden treasure inside is hid" (Tolkien, 2011, 71). Through these verses, the Hobbit managed to open an even greater hole in the dark life of the Stoor. In fact:

> But it proved a nasty poser for Gollum. He hissed to himself, and still he did not answer; he whispered and spluttered. […] But suddenly Gollum remembered thieving from nests long ago, and sitting under the river bank teaching his grandmother, teaching his grandmother to suck – "Eggses!" he hissed. "Eggses it is!" (72)

As much as Gollum tried to bring everything back to the oblivion of his darkness, in reality, life had regained possession of his memories. A riddle concerning an object of simple everyday life such as "eggs" was enough to bring back a memory with a sweet fragrance, full of those scents and that familiar warmth that had allowed a dark and cold cave to 'magically' transform itself, even just for an instant, into that house by the river where he had taught his grandmother to suck that 'golden treasure' contained in such a precious casket.

5. Gollum's grandmother: the most important female memory in Middle-earth

Even Gollum's grandmother is one of the most important female figures of Middle-earth and the stories of the Third Age told in *The Hobbit* and *The Lord of the Rings*. Recalling the fact that Gollum had taught his grandmother to suck eggs,

Tolkien used a pun and idiom dear to English culture and placed it in a completely different narrative context (Tolkien, 2017a, 140, notes 21).

This allowed a whole new world to open up before the reader: the daily life of a particular race of the Hobbits, namely the Stoors. In *The Lord of the Rings*, Gandalf provided some more information about them. He told Frodo that, in ancient times, there was a small people in Wilderland, ancestors of the Hobbits, where a "large and wealthy family" lived. Sméagol and his grandmother were part of this family. She was the breadwinner and was "stern and wise in old lore". Instead, Sméagol "was the most inquisitive and curious-minded of his family". He loved "roots and beginnings". But, taking possession of the ring, he received a power commensurate with his stature. He began to commit misdeeds and was gradually isolated from all his relatives and family members (Tolkien, 2005, 52-53). Of this, Gandalf said: "So they called him *Gollum*, and cursed him, and told him to go far away; and his grandmother, desiring peace, expelled him from the family and turned him out of her hole" (53-54).

Therefore, it can be said that there is a red thread connecting the ring (later discovered to be the Ring of Power), Sméagol (later to become Gollum), and his grandmother (that is, the great progenitor and expert in the ancient traditions of her race). The relationship between these three then led to the events which, subsequently, would see Bilbo and Frodo as protagonists.

But what would have happened if Gollum, not meeting the ring, hadn't been chased away from his grandmother and his native village? What soul would Gollum have had if he hadn't allowed himself to be corrupted by the ring? What would have happened if he had continued to spend more time in the sun and by the river with his grandmother instead of holed up in the dark and cold caves of the Misty Mountains?

The answer to these and other similar questions is impossible to give. But one thing is certain: if all this had happened, we would not have had the adventures of Tolkien's novels nor have met a character as fascinating as Gollum.

However, there is an even stronger element that binds the Ring, Gollum and his grandmother. This element was explained once again by Gandalf to Frodo:

> Gollum is a liar [...]. For instance, he called the Ring his "birthday-present", and he stuck to that. He said it came from his grandmother, who had lots of beautiful things of that kind. A ridiculous story. I have no doubt that Sméagol's grandmother was a matriarch, a great person in her way, but to talk of her possessing many Elven-rings was absurd, and as for giving them away, it was a lie. But a lie with a grain of truth. (56)

This last sentence is very interesting. In his story, Gandalf considered what Gollum had told him about his "birthday-present": a lie which, at its core, also contained "a grain of truth". He was probably referring here to the fact that, in the first edition of *The Hobbit*, in which Gollum was less evil and not a liar, it was stated that the ring was a gift to the Stoor on his birthday. Therefore, the claim that his grandmother possessed many riches and had given her grandson the ring could possibly be considered true.

However, from the point of view of the second edition, this reconstruction was a blatant lie. Actually, the reader now knows how Sméagol came into possession of his 'Preciousss', i.e. through the killing of his cousin Déagol.

In light of all this, whether it was a complete lie or a partial truth, this statement by the Stoor to Gandalf allows the reader to see the importance and central role of Gollum's grandmother in the life of both her grandson and the whole of Middle-earth.

This is particularly evident in a long draft of letter n. 214, probably written between the end of 1958 and the beginning of 1959. In it, Tolkien tried to explain some things about Stoors to A.C. Nunn, who had enquired about the Hobbits' custom of giving and receiving gifts on their birthdays. In this letter, the Professor wrote this about Gollum and his grandmother:

> [* I imagine that he was an orphan; and do not suppose that he *gave* any present on his birthday, save (grudgingly) the tribute to his 'grandmother']. […] Gandalf's use (or rather his reporter and translator's use) of the word 'matriarch' was not 'anthropological', but meant simply a woman who in fact ruled the clan. No doubt because she had outlived her husband, and was a woman of dominant character. It is likely enough that, in the recessive and decadent Stoor-country of Wilderland, the women-folk (as is often to be observed in such conditions) tended to preserve better the physical and mental character of the past, and so became of special importance. (Tolkien, 2006c, 292-296)

This letter allows the reader to better understand, in a clearer way, the family and Sméagol's existential story. In fact, through the description of the tradition of gifts among the Hobbits in general, and among the Stoors in particular, Tolkien managed to draw a very clear picture of this race of creatures which also allows the reader to understand why and how Sméagol became Gollum. Actually, the social and cultural environment in which this being had grown up was indeed one of a good and well-to-do family but inserted in a context that had become totally decayed, barely civilised and, in any case, retrograde compared to the Hobbits of the Shire.

Sméagol too, like Frodo, was probably an orphan who, however, had a conflicting relationship with his relatives: while Frodo wanted to find his uncle Bilbo and stay with him, Sméagol had reluctantly paid tribute to his grandmother, though it had occurred to him almost as the only distant memory from his past, during the guessing contest with Bilbo.

Unfortunately, very little space has been given to this dominant character by critics of Tolkien's use of female figures in Middle-earth. In my opinion, she carries a decisive importance both for the development of the story of the Ring and for the role of women in the Professor's stories. In fact, she had assumed the responsibility of looking after and raising Sméagol in the best possible way.

We do not know what the real relationship between grandmother and grandson was. The only certain thing is that this "matriarch" was Sméagol's only family, the only "light out of the past" (Tolkien, 2005, 55) that touched his heart and mind again. Thanks to Bilbo and some 'riddles in the dark', Gollum, an ignoble Stoor who was a prisoner of his own darkness, was slowly managing to escape from the black prison which he himself had taken refuge in so long ago.

Chapter 3

Gollum And The Lord Of The Rings: "My Preciousss"

1. The narrative genesis of Gollum and Sméagol in *The Lord of the Rings*

In the mid-fifties of the last century, *The Lord of the Rings* first saw the light of day. While Tolkien was crafting his narrative masterpiece, he also told something of Gollum and the evolution of this character in some letters. For example, in a note on letter n. 35 of 2nd February 1939 addressed to C. Furth, he wrote: "Still there are more hobbits, far more of them and about them, in the new story. Gollum reappears, and Gandalf is to the fore" (Tolkien, 2006c, 42). Or, in letter n. 70 of 21st May 1944, referred to his son, Christopher: "Gollum continues to develop into a most intriguing character" (81).

After the publication of *The Lord of the Rings*, the readers were confronted with a figure never seen before and strongly connected to Gollum, namely Sméagol. He was introduced through a tale told by Gandalf to Frodo in the chapter 'The Shadow of the Past' in *The Fellowship of the Ring* (Tolkien, 2005, 52-54).

In it, the Wizard told the origin of this miserable creature who was passionate about roots and origins and, for this reason, he always had his head turned downwards. No longer accustomed to the presence of the sun and to looking at the leaves and the trees, he had chosen as his home the caves beneath the Misty Mountains.

All this provoked a series of questions in readers that can be traced in the answers that Tolkien provided in his letters. In fact, in draft letter n. 156 of 4th November 1954, writing to his Jesuit friend Father Robert Murray, who had made some comments on *The Lord of the Rings*, the Professor stated: "No, 'Sméagol' was not, of course, fully envisaged at first, but I believe his character was implicit, and merely needed attention" (Tolkien, 2006c, 201).

Furthermore, in the draft letter n. 181 of January-February 1956 addressed to Michael Straight, speaking about Gollum, Tolkien wrote:

> Gollum is to me just a 'character' – an imagined person – who granted the situation acted so and so under opposing strains, as it appears to be *probable* that he would (there is always an incalculable element in any individual real or imagined: otherwise he/she would not be an individual but a 'type') […] Into the ultimate judgement upon Gollum I would not care to enquire. [...] Gollum was pitiable, but he ended in persistent wickedness, and the fact that this worked good was no credit to him. His marvellous courage and endurance [...] being devoted to evil was portentous, but not honourable. [...] We have to face the fact that there are persons who yield to temptation, reject their chances of nobility or salvation, and appear to be 'damnable'. Their 'damnability' is *not* measurable in the terms of the macrocosm (where it may work good). But we who are all 'in the same boat' must not usurp the Judge. The domination of the Ring was much too strong for the mean soul of Sméagol. But he would have never had to endure it if he had not become a mean sort of thief before it crossed his path. [...] By temporizing, not fixing the still not wholly corrupt Sméagol-will towards good in the debate

in the slag hole, he weakened himself for the final chance when dawning love of Frodo was too easily withered by the jealousy of Sam before Shelob's lair. After that he was lost. (233-235)

These words are essential to understanding Gollum and moving away from the vision of this character as a schizophrenic, a bipolar, a symbol of the internal struggle between good and evil, or between light and shadow. What emerges from this letter, in Tolkien's mind, is that Sméagol and Gollum were not two distinct people nor, even more, two separate parts: Gollum was simply the 'extreme Sméagol'.

The wickedness and pettiness he already possessed within himself due to his soul, his existential experience, and the social context which he had grown up in, contributed to bringing him to exasperation and excess through the darkness of the Ring.

In Tolkien's stories, evil is not capable of creating anything. Instead, if the person allows it to thrive by not exercising ethical virtue, or by not persevering in a moral path dedicated to good, it could attach itself in a parasitic way to human weaknesses, pettiness, and frailties, causing the 'damnation', the consumption and the near-annihilation of the subject.

This is evident in draft letter n. 212 of 1958 addressed to Rhona Beare:

To attempt by device or 'magic' to recover longevity is thus a supreme folly and wickedness of 'mortals'. Longevity or counterfeit 'immortality' (true immortality is beyond Eä) is the chief bait of Sauron – it leads the small to a Gollum, and the great to a Ringwraith. (286)

The contents of this sentence are fundamental to the last part of our journey, when it comes to Gollum's death. What is of interest here is showing that the Ring, Middle-earth's greatest and most perfidious technological weapon, had led Sméagol, a miserable Stoor, to such a state of despair, withdrawal and exasperation, as to cause him to become 'a Gollum', a desperate and despicable creature.

The relationship between the Ring and Sméagol is masterfully told by Gandalf to Frodo in the continuation of their dialogue in the second chapter of *The Lord of the Rings*. By reconstructing Gollum's poignant story, the Wizard showed that there was a before and after for Bilbo's theft of Gollum's 'Precious'.

In fact, Gandalf stressed that it was actually the Ring making decisions and not Gollum. This evil object had consumed the Stoor to the point that he no longer had any willpower. He could no longer free himself from the spell of the Ring he loved and hated at the same time, because it was now part of himself: Gollum called both himself and the Ring 'precious'.

Therefore, using a purely juridical definition, he was '*non compos sui*'; that is, he was not a master of himself. His ability to understand and want had been greatly affected, even if some glimmer of light could still penetrate. Indeed, in his account, Gandalf made it clear to Frodo that Gollum was not a hopeless case. For this reason, Bilbo's presence in those caves, through his voice and his kind ways, had managed to bring everything that existed outside those underground caves back to the Stoor's mind: that is, water, wind, sun, meadows and daisies.

However, beauty, tenderness and kindness had made the evil part of Gollum's soul wicked. Attention must be paid to this detail: Tolkien, in this case, did not affirm that Gollum was the evil part and Sméagol the good and nostalgic part. Instead, the Professor wanted to underline an evident reality: often, the human soul, faced with goodness and kindness, reacts in a harsh and malignant way, as it is aware of its own meanness and being undeserving of that kindness.

In fact, from the moment that Bilbo stole the Ring from Gollum – i.e. in the *The Hobbit* – until the end of *The Lord of the Rings*, the reader is faced with only Gollum (i.e. the 'extreme Sméagol') having escaped from the cold dark caves in which he was locked up.

In all of this, Tolkien acutely communicated how the lust and power of the Ring led Gollum on a new moral and existential journey. The creature which emerged from the caves of the Misty Mountains, who had faced the journey first to Mirkwood and then to Mondor, was very different from the one previously written by Tolkien. Actually, although he was still attracted by the Ring which was now in Bilbo's pocket, Gollum was no longer devoured by it, but had instead begun to 'revive'.

This new awareness resulting from the reappropriation of himself and his own will, and returning to being '*compos sui*', albeit still marked and influenced by the evil attraction of the Ring, had made all the memories of the past re-emerge in an overwhelming and painful way, including those of his grandmother and Déagol's murder.

It was precisely Déagol's murder that Gollum had become obsessed with, seeking alibis and excuses in order to avoid admitting what he had done years earlier. To render the turmoil within Gollum's soul into a clear image, one could say that he was similar to someone who has been sedated for surgery and then, as the anesthesia slowly wears off, feels all their pain resurfacing.

Gollum had to deal with exactly such a condition: he had killed his best friend for reasons of self-interest and selfishness. In fact, on the basis of Tolkien's words in his letters, and in light of his stories, it can be affirmed that Déagol's murder had not been caused by the evil influence of the Ring, but instead by the fact that a Hobbit was easily pleased by a pleasant, or unexpectedly 'good', gift.

Therefore, the guilt of that murder didn't come from outside his soul but from within him. Its origin lay in the desire to possess an object that was beautiful, glittering, desirable to the eye, and which was more precious than the 'miserable' gift previously given to him by Déagol.

However, Gollum sought alibis and justifications: he knew that it wasn't Sauron's power that had led him to kill his closest friend. Instead, the Stoor knew it was his own fault, caused by the greed and evil that were already present in him and had simply emerged, for the sake of self-interest, in such a petty, violent and tragic way.

2. Sméagol or Gollum: which character in Tolkien's works?

To correctly analyse the relationship between Sméagol and Gollum, it is necessary to start with two fundamental assumptions. The first is of a general nature and concerns the identity of the character that the reader finds in the tales of *The Hobbit* and *The Lord of the Rings*. So two questions arise: who did Bilbo meet in the caves of the Misty Mountains? And who guided Frodo and Sam to Mordor? The simplest and most correct way to answer these questions is to look at what is stated by the narrator of the story.

Through *Appendix B*, concerning 'The Tale of Years' (Tolkien, 2005, 1087-1094), with indisputable precision, Tolkien demonstrated the existence of no less than three phases of Gollum's story within the Third Age of Middle-earth:

a) The first phase is that of *Sméagol* from 2463 to 2470 (during which the Stoor came to be hidden in the Misty Mountains);

b) The second phase is that of *Sméagol-Gollum* from 2470 to 2944 (during which Bilbo met this wretched creature in the caves of the Misty Mountains in 2941);

c) The third phase is that of *Gollum* from 2944 to 25th March 3019 (the day of his death at Mount Doom).

From this simple schema it is possible to note that, as I have tried to demonstrate above, Déagol's murder was committed in 2463 by Sméagol, independent of the Ring's influence.

However, that evil object had then become his 'Precious' and begun to corrode him internally, causing his total isolation, a serial longevity and the gradual extremization of his more negative attributes. This is the Sméagol-Gollum transition period. At this hybrid moment, Bilbo had fallen into meeting the creature in the caves of the Misty Mountains which, in *The Hobbit*, is called the 'old Gollum'.

The Stoor's awareness of having lost his 'birthday present' and the fact that it was the Hobbit himself who had stolen it from him, had brought the extremization of his soul to its final act: this was Gollum's moment. Crying out for vengeance and coming out of his underground lair, he had now become an undisputed main character, together with Frodo and Sam, in *The Lord of the Rings*.

All this is confirmed by a statement found in the chapter, 'The Taming of Sméagol', from *The Two Towers*, within a dialogue between Frodo and Gollum concerning the necessity for going to Mordor:

> Gollum sat up again and looked at him under his eyelids. 'He's over there,' he cackled. 'Always there. Orcs will take you all the way. Easy to find Orcs east of the River. Don't ask Sméagol. Poor, poor Sméagol, he went away long ago. They took his Precious, and he is lost now'.
> 'Perhaps we'll find him again, if you come with us,' said Frodo.
> 'No, no, never! He's lost his Precious,' said Gollum. (616)

In light of the *Appendix*, it is easier to interpret this dialogue between the two Hobbits. Conversely, Gollum's words confirm what was said in 'The Tale of Years'. In this dialogue, the acting and speaking character is 'Gollum'. He had told Frodo not to ask Sméagol to be his guide towards Mordor because "he went away a long time ago". This sentence can be interpreted in two ways: either as an affirmation that Sméagol had set out in search of the Ring and then landed in Mordor; or that the Stoor, Sméagol, that is to say what Gollum had been before the arrival of his "Preciousss", was no longer there, had vanished, had gone away.

This second hypothesis is supported by what Gollum himself said: namely that, having stolen the Ring, Sméagol "is lost now". This statement was followed by Frodo's words: "Perhaps we'll find him again, if you come with us".

The interpretation of these words can be of two types: on the one hand, it could indicate a simple ploy by Frodo to gain the goodwill of Gollum and, therefore, induce him to be their guide towards Mordor; on the other hand, a second, perhaps more correct interpretation, could be that Frodo was telling Gollum to share the road with them because he really was worried about bringing out the Stoor that was hidden beneath the meanness of that miserable creature again. Through this sharing and walking together in that 'little company of the Ring', it would have been possible to find Sméagol again, without the extremes and desire for revenge that were characteristic of Gollum.

Here, Tolkien has shown in a narrative way what was then listed schematically in 'The Tale of Years'. Once the Ring had been stolen, 'Sméagol' had also gone with it and only 'Gollum' was left. Since then, he was no longer a Stoor, but a miserable creature who, however, through Frodo's empathy, had been able to rediscover the possibility of making the 'lost Sméagol' resurface and return to existence.

3. Gollum: a journey full of changes

Actually, Frodo was right: the journey to Mordor had managed to dent Gollum's monolithic evil soul; this 'extreme Sméagol', a creature now emaciated in body, with an unnatural longevity, who possessed all the characteristics of malice and wickedness already present in the Stoor who had killed Déagol. He had been corroded by his possession of the Ring which, moreover, had been stolen from him and provoked in him a single thought: to reappropriate his 'Preciousss', while taking revenge on Bilbo and all the Baggins.

However, during this story, something totally unexpected had happened: the meeting between this miserable creature and Frodo. The Hobbit started calling Gollum by his old name, Sméagol, rekindling in him an ancient spark, which he considered almost completely extinguished. Frodo had breached the world of darkness and vengeance that was Gollum's heart. The empathy shown by this Hobbit had worked hard and persistently in the Stoor's mind and soul. This provoked what unfolded in a crucial moment contained in the chapter 'The Taming of Sméagol', in *The Two Towers*. In it, after Frodo had ordered Sam to free Gollum from the grip of the rope he was tied with, this happened:

> From that moment a change [...] came over him. He spoke with less hissing and whining, and he spoke to his companions direct, not to his precious self. [...] He was friendly, and indeed pitifully anxious to please. He would cackle with laughter and caper, if any jest was made, or even if Frodo spoke kindly to him [...]. Sam [...] suspected him more deeply than ever, and if possible liked the new Gollum, the Sméagol, less than the old. (Tolkien, 2005, 618-619)

Thus, a radical and important change had taken place in Gollum's life: he once again enjoyed the beauty not only of living in the sun but also of sharing something with another. In fact, Gollum suffered from extreme existential loneliness to the point of calling himself 'precious'. However, once he returned to social interactions, he slowly began to address his companions directly, without the aid of the third person.

This situation caused an emotional imbalance in him: he was now capable of sympathy for others, experiencing their own *pathos*, even going so far as to laugh with them. This change is visible through the name 'Sméagol', now presented as the 'new Gollum' i.e. a creature re-socialised and refined by the mercy and delicacy of someone similar him: Frodo.

Therefore, it is possible to delineate in these terms the essential relationship between Gollum and Sméagol: Gollum was 'the extreme Sméagol' and Sméagol was 'the new loved and re-socialised Gollum'. This inseparable identity between Gollum and Sméagol – that cannot be qualified as schizophrenia or psychiatric pathology, nor as a Manichaean symbol of the struggle between good and evil, or light and shadow – is also well expressed in the title of the chapter in which all this is shown: 'The taming of Sméagol'. This shows a direct reference to the passage in which Gollum is described as a kind of pet, faithful to his master Frodo, who calls him Sméagol, and no longer Gollum.

Obviously this change, being one in progress, was also bumpy, full of obstacles and difficulties. For instance, in the chapter 'The Passage of the Marshes' in *The Two Towers*, it is said that: "At the word *hungry* a greenish light was kindled in Gollum's pale eyes, and they seemed to protrude further than ever from his thin sickly face. For a moment he relapsed into his old Gollum-manner" (622). To this must be added a further modification of his soul, which is told in this way in the same chapter:

> From that time on Sam thought that he sensed a change in Gollum again. He was more fawning and would-be friendly;

> but Sam surprised some strange looks in his eyes at times, especially towards Frodo; and he went back more and more into his old manner of speaking. (630)

The Ringwraiths, the violence suffered in Mordor, the fear of Sauron – that Dark Lord who from time to time resurfaced in his memories – getting ever closer to that infernal and cursed land, had made all the wickedness re-emerge in Gollum and the meanness in his being. However, now this internal situation had collided with Gollum's awareness that someone cared about him and also that he had promised to guide the two Hobbits towards Mordor.

The inner anguish was growing. Sam had witnessed all of this and the changes that had taken place in Gollum. Although often he could not understand what exactly was changing in the Stoor's soul, he had nevertheless sensed that something would happen sooner or later. Indeed, as will be seen in the next paragraph, an internal debate between Sméagol and Gollum managed to pierce the deafening silence of a dark night in Middle-earth.

4. Gollum, Frodo and Sam: from a 'stealth touch' to a 'warm caress'

At the beginning of this chapter, I recalled a passage from a Tolkien letter which it is now time to analyse in more detail. Actually, it allows the reader to better understand an intratextual connection which, otherwise, would risk being lost. The reference is to draft letter n. 181 of January-February 1956 addressed to Michael Straight:

> The domination of the Ring was much too strong for the mean soul of Sméagol. [...] By temporizing, not fixing the still not wholly corrupt Sméagol-will towards good in the debate in the slag hole. (Tolkien, 2006c, 234-235)

From this text, it is possible to obtain two very precise indications which must be evaluated separately. The first concerns a concept that, on the basis of the Catholic tradition, Tolkien possessed regarding moral action as a path in which it is necessary to engage one's will in the search for good, albeit in the awareness of being able to also give in, abandoning oneself to evil and stubbornly pursuing it. This is evident in letter n. 183 from 1956 containing some notes about the review of *The Return of the King* by W.H. Auden, in which it is emphasised that:

> A man is both a seed and in some degree also a gardener [...]. I am impressed by the degree in which the development of 'character' *can* be a product of conscious intention, the will to modify innate tendencies in desired directions. (240)

Therefore, Gollum, by not committing himself to modifying his own 'innate malice' and 'unkindness', had not set out on a moral path that would have led to him changing his life and returning to his own goodness and that of others. Once again, Tolkien demonstrated that Gollum was not mentally ill but, on the contrary, he was a subject with well-developed cognitive and volitional abilities but directed towards a horizon of wickedness rather than benevolence and love.

On the basis of this, it is necessary to make a second consideration arising from the text of the aforementioned draft letter: namely, the existence of a conceptual and narrative link between the debate between Sméagol and Gollum in the slag hole and that of Sam's abrupt reaction against him before Shelob's lair.

4.1 A 'stealthy touch' in the debate between Sméagol and Gollum in the slag hole

The first of the two episodes to deal with is contained in the chapter 'The Passage of the Marshes' in *The Two Towers*. It recounts the capture of Gollum by Sam and the pity Frodo showed towards this miserable creature.

The conceptual context in which this part of *The Lord of the Rings* is situated is a 'triadic order'. In fact, Tolkien seems to have used a schema whose main points could be listed as follows:

1) Thought (or will);
2) Voice (or word);
3) Action (or touch).

This schema was constructed by the author in a consequential and logical way: a character first 'thought' (or wanted) something, which they then expressed verbally (through their own or another 'voice') and, finally, 'acted' on.

Taking this into account, it is easier to understand the events in the slag hole. It has already been said that the journey to Mordor had led Gollum to a series of changes that he could never have imagined.

One of these modifications concerned his 'thought'. In fact, the character 'Gollum' had a 'single thought': to find the

Ring at all costs, even by killing any thieves of his 'Precious', especially Bilbo and Frodo. This thought was so all-encompassing that he spoke in the plural – in a sort of *pluralis maiestatis* – hissing and squealing in a low and frightening way.

However, Frodo's empathy for him and the journey together with the two Hobbits had brought Gollum to 'another thought' – i.e. another way of reasoning and seeing things – which Tolkien called 'Sméagol'. This thought possessed a different voice to Gollum and often spoke in the first person singular. Also, while the 'thought Gollum' had tried to touch Frodo to find and steal the Ring, 'the thought Sméagol' withdrew his hand from the master of his 'Precious'.

Thus, in Gollum there had been a transition from a 'single thought' – which possessed a single typology of voice and action – to the coexistence in the same person of a 'plurality of thoughts and ways of reasoning' – which had prompted him to take account of himself, with his past, and his goals and objectives.

In fact, in the slag hole, a genuine internal diatribe had taken place in Gollum. This inner struggle is common to all people who are faced with fundamental choices in their lives and, not knowing what to do, find themselves having to face numerous thoughts and options, and indecision reigns supreme.

In this case, the 'Gollum thought' desired the Ring at all costs, even considering the possibility of killing Frodo. To win the inner battle, this way of reasoning had resorted to vainglory, imagining the most diverse denominations that he could have once he possessed the Ring: "Lord Sméagol? Gollum the Great? *The* Gollum!" (Tolkien, 2005, 633).

The first two terms, "Lord" and "the Great", are the same appellations of Sauron. Actually, he was defined as "the Dark Lord" and "Sauron the Great". If these two terms are of the interrogative voice, the third one is witnessed in an exclamation. Indeed, "*The* Gollum!" recalls the name of the Ring of Power: '*The* Ring'. This creates an absolute identification between the owner and the possessed object.

Instead, the 'Sméagol thought', while sharing the desire to regain possession of the Ring – which was therefore common to both thoughts – had accepted the idea of having 'another way of reasoning', far from any form of violence or killing Frodo.

However, what is the reason for all this? One hypothesis could be that the 'Sméagol thought' brought with him the memory of the past, his suffering due to loneliness and, above all, the agony and the remorse of having killed Déagol. It is as if the 'Gollum thought' had considered killing Frodo because he did not know what it meant to kill a friend. Instead, the 'Sméagol thought' knew this feeling well because, when Déagol died, there was only him, and the 'Gollum thought' had not yet appeared.

In short, what many authors maintain about the relationship between Gollum and Frodo is true: the Stoor and the Hobbit mirrored each other. But a further relationship can be added to this, perhaps even more profound and painful: the 'Sméagol thought' saw, in Frodo, his old friend Déagol, the last person who had used his original Stoor name, exactly as, since the beginning of their acquaintance, Frodo had done.

However, in this intense and heartbreaking debate, a 'third thought' had appeared, a 'third way of reasoning' that had brought the other two thoughts together, removing all their responsability.

In fact, in this context, failing to decide what to do, Gollum had entrusted the fate of Frodo to 'She': that is, a third subject that Sam had not been able to clearly identify, but that the reader knows to be the spider Shelob. In this evil plan, She would have the task of killing Frodo, allowing Gollum to act undisturbed and re-appropriate his 'Precious'.

It is interesting to understand how, in Tolkien's mind, the idea of this giant female Spider came about. In letter n. 144 of 25th April 1954 addressed to Naomi Mitchison, it is explained that:

> Shelob (English representing C.S 'she-lob' = female spider) is a translation of Elvish *Ungol* 'spider'. She is represented in vol. II p. 332 as descendant of the giant spiders of the glens of *Nandungorthin*, which come into the legends of the First Age, especially into the chief of them, the tale of Beren and Lúthien. (Tolkien, 2006c, 180)

So, Tolkien had inserted this disgusting and terrible female spider as a reassuring and reconciling 'third thought' in the mind of Gollum who, therefore, could continue his journey totally devoid of responsibility for Frodo's safety.

On the basis of all this, the Professor's words can be understood more clearly in the draft letter n. 181 of 1956 addressed to Michael Straight:

> By temporizing, not fixing the still not wholly corrupt Sméagol-will towards good in the debate in the slag hole, he weakened himself for the final chance when dawning love of

Frodo was too easily withered by the jealousy of Sam before Shelob's lair. After that he was lost. (Tolkien, 2006c, 235)

The episode at Shelob's lair will be the subject of the next paragraph, because it is closely connected to what has been said so far. However, there is a substantial difference between them: near the house of this large female spider, the hand that Gollum would extend towards Frodo's body was no longer that of a 'furtive touch' to steal the Ring, but rather an 'affectionate caress' for his dear master.

4.2 An 'affectionate caress' in front of Shelob's lair

Sam, together with Gollum, are the focal characters of the second piece which structures a kind of narrative diptych, whose extremes are the two 'touches' of the Stoor, albeit in a completely different way. The story is told in the chapter 'The Stairs of Cirith Ungol' in *The Two Towers*. In it, the two Hobbits and Gollum are almost at the finishing line of Shelob's Lair. Sam and Frodo fell asleep and:

> Gollum looked at them. A strange expression passedover his lean hungry face. The gleam faded from his eyes, and they went dim and grey, old and tired. A spasm of pain seemed to twist him, and he turned away, peering back up toward the pass, shaking his head, as if engaged in some interior debate. Then he came back, and slowly putting out a trembling hand, very cautiously he touched Frodo's knee – but almost the touch was a caress. For a fleeting moment, could one of the sleepers have seen him, they would have thought that they beheld an old weary hobbit, shrunken by the years that had

carried him far beyond his time, beyond friends and kin, and the fields and streams of youth, an old starved pitiable thing. But at that touch Frodo stirred and cried out softly in his sleep, and immediately Sam was wide awake. The first thing he saw was Gollum – 'pawing at master,' as he thought. 'Hey you!' he said roughly […]. Gollum withdrew himself, and a green glint flickered under his heavy lids. […] The fleeting moment had passed, beyond recall. (Tolkien, 2005, 714-715)

Tolkien, commenting on this scene, thus wrote to his son Christopher in letter n. 96 of 30th January 1945:

For myself, I was prob. most moved by Sam's disquisition on the seamless web of story, and by the scene when Frodo goes to sleep on his breast, and the tragedy of Gollum who at that moment came within a hair of repentance – but for one rough word from Sam. (Tolkien, 2006c, 110)

Or in letter n. 165 of 1955 intended for the Houghton Mifflin Co., thus the author confided:

I am […] most grieved by Gollum's failure (just) to repent when interrupted by Sam: this seems to me really like the *real* world in which the instruments of just retribution are seldom themselves just or holy; and the good are often stumbling blocks. (221)

Or again in draft letter n. 246 of September 1963 addressed to Mrs. Eileen Elgar, speaking about Sam, thus the Professor wrote: "For me perhaps the most tragic moment in the Tale comes in II 323 ff. when Sam fails to note the complete change in Gollum's tone and aspect" (330).

In light of what is told in the story and these letters, it is clear that the two points around which the narration was built concern, on the one hand, the change that took place in Gollum and, on the other, the impossibility of bringing his life path to full fruition as a result of Sam's vehemence and jealousy.

The general picture that frames all this is similar to, in an almost specular sense, the episode in the slag hole. In fact, in this case too, as in the previous one, Sam and Frodo had fallen asleep while Gollum, who was once again in the throes of an inner struggle, remained awake and near his master. Also, here too, Sam, waking up, had seen the miserable creature reach out to Frodo. If these are the similarities within this story, there are, however, some substantial differences that allow the reader to understand both Gollum's change and Sam's reaction.

With regards to the first point, no one will ever know the subject of the debate that took place within Gollum. Only the cause (i.e. the fact that he had seen Frodo and Sam sleeping, embracing) and the consequence (i.e. the changes in Gollum's eyes and appearance, and the way he pats Frodo's knee) are understood.

Who knows if, at that moment, Gollum had returned to being Sméagol or if he was undergoing an even more radical change, discarding even the unkindness already present in the young, murderous Stoor. Tolkien does not say as much, but he causes the reader to perceive how something was completely changing in that unhappy creature's soul.

In fact, Gollum, thanks to Frodo's empathy, had rediscovered the joy of being part of a community, of being an 'old Hobbit' who was certainly alone and far from affection, from his family, from the places of his youth, but who was also discovering the beauty of walking together, side by side, in friendship.

This was absolutely not perceived or understood by Sam. In this regard, one sentence within the analysed passage is symptomatic:

> For a fleeting moment, could one of the sleepers have seen him, they would have thought that they beheld an old weary hobbit, shrunken by the years that had carried him far beyond his time, beyond friends and kin, and the fields and streams of youth, an old starved pitiable thing. (Tolkien, 2005, 714-715)

However, a few lines later, we are told what actually happened: one of the two Hobbits had woken up and had an opposite reaction to the one previously foreseen by the narrator.

The question to be asked concerns the reason for this evident inconsistency. The answer may lie in the fact that Sam had previously been the only witness to the internal Gollum debate in the slag hole: in that case, the 'Gollum thought' (or, as he called it, 'Stinker') emerging in the Stoor's soul, had reached out to Frodo to rummage and try to get the Ring.

So, these were the parameters which Sam had in his mind. Having missed Gollum's second internal debate and not knowing which of his two inclinations had taken hold of the Stoor's mind, he assumed that 'Stinker' was reaching out his hand to Frodo in the same manner he had in the slag hole.

However, Sam hadn't realised that what he was observing was no longer a 'furtive touch', but instead an 'affectionate caress'. In fact, within these two touches, there lies all of Gollum's existential journey, all of his inner anguish, and his newfound desire to live together with others.

In order to perceive all this, Sam would have had to open his heart to Gollum and open wide his spirit to what was seemingly debased and disagreeable. Sam did not possess all that, enclosed as he was in his prejudices towards Gollum, and his morbid jealousy due to his devotion to Frodo. He was unable to fully understand his master and follow him in his gradual education of nobility in service to the unlovable. If only he had done this, Sam could have perceived the goodness which was hidden within the corrupt and vile Gollum.

5. Gollum: the ignoble 'sought', 'pursued' and 'found' by Pity and Mercy

In light of all that has been said up to now, it can be asserted that Gollum was a traitor, a thief, a liar, a perjurer, a murderer who, albeit in searching for his 'Precious', had accepted the challenge of confrontation, of going out in the open, of no longer hiding in safe lairs under the Mountains. He was slowly returning to daily life, to the surface of the real world and knew he was risking his life because he could encounted enemies even stronger than him – such as Sauron and Shelob – who could crush him or plunge him even further into darkness.

But this miserable creature had also allowed Pity and Mercy into his life, through the eyes, words, and gestures of Hobbits and Men who had shared his journey in Middle-earth to Mordor.

They had succeeded in dilating his heart to such an extent as to create in him, even if only for a moment, the desire to change his life and to love again. Emerging from his lair, Gollum had begun an extraordinary new moral and existential adventure.

In fact, if Frodo can be considered as an exemplification or personification of the 'humble accompanied and supported by grace', Gollum is certainly the exemplification or personification of the 'ignoble who was sought, pursued and found by Pity and Mercy'.

But Gollum did not embrace the gestures of Pity and Mercy towards him, nor surrender to them with confidence, allowing himself to be saved and transformed internally. The greatest tragedy in this creature's story can be found in his stubbornness and obstinacy.

On the basis of all this, it is possible to understand more fully and clearly the words of the aforementioned draft letter n. 181 of January-February 1956 addressed to Michael Straight:

> I am afraid, whatever our beliefs, we have to face the fact that there are persons who yield to temptation, reject their chances of nobility or salvation, and appear to be 'damnable'. Their 'damnability' is *not* measurable in the terms of the macrocosm (where it may work good). But we who are all 'in the same boat' must not usurp the Judge. (Tolkien, 2066c, 234)

Tolkien, despite being the sub-creator of Middle-earth, had decided not to judge his characters morally and spiritually or, above all, Gollum's miserable life: only the great Judge, i.e. Eru, could have assumed this right.

Instead, the Professor, a man in the same boat as his imaginary character, limited himself to contemplating this petty and miserable creature, feeling Pity and Mercy for him, as many protagonists in his stories had done, hoping until the last moment for his repentance.

5.1 Gollum and Bilbo: between Pity and Mercy

The first character who took Pity and Mercy on Gollum was Bilbo. This is told in Chapter V, 'Riddles in the Dark' in *The Hobbit*, during their meeting in the Misty Mountains' caves (Tolkien, 2011, 81-84). In it, it is interesting to note the change in Bilbo's attitude towards Gollum.

Indeed, initially the Hobbit had had an attitude of refusal, detachment and little compassion and pity for the Stoor. This is a common trait found in all characters who meet Gollum thereafter.

However, despite their initial refusal, all of Bilbo, Sam and Frodo changed their attitude towards him. This was due to the fact that all these three characters had been able to gain a deep insight into Gollum and, like him, wore the Ring of Power. Therefore, they were able to understand what it could mean for such a miserable and desperate creature to lose his 'Precious'.

In fact, a clear change in Bilbo's soul can be noticed. If, in the beginning, the Hobbit's will had been to kill Gollum, it then transformed into ethical and almost 'deontological' correctness: that is, respect for the formal rules of a duel on equal terms.

Actually, in the last remnants of the episode between the Hobbit and the Stoor, Bilbo had the Ring on his finger and this put him in an advantageous position: not only could Gollum not see it but, conversely, Bilbo could see Gollum's depth better and more closely. So, this reversal of roles provoked a sudden understanding in the Hobbit, allowing Bilbo to imagine himself in the same miserable condition as Gollum, in which all the comforts of Bag End no longer existed, and instead there was only dark, cold, despair and a lack of any perspective and future.

Besides, Bilbo understood that Gollum was alone, without friends or relatives, without a gentle voice that could touch his heart, which had become so withered. Once again, the theme of Gollum's solitude had risen to the surface from the gloom which Bilbo had leaped across in all its fullness.

Thus, the pity that Bilbo showed brought compassion and mercy to an ignoble and petty character like Gollum. However, Tolkien went one step further than this event.

In fact, in *The Lord of the Rings*, there is a kind of authentic interpretation of this meeting between Bilbo and Gollum, referenced by Gandalf in his conversation with Frodo in the chapter 'The Shadow of the Past':

> Cried Frodo […]: 'What a pity that Bilbo did not stab that vile creature, when he had a chance!'. 'Pity? It was Pity that stayed his hand. Pity, and Mercy: not to strike without need. And he has been well rewarded, Frodo. Be sure that he took so little hurt from the evil, and escaped in the end, because he began his ownership of the Ring so. With Pity'. (Tolkien, 2005, 59)

In this dialogue, Gandalf tried to show Frodo the other side of the coin: the attitude that Bilbo had towards Gollum had not been negative, but an act of proper 'Pity' (with a capital letter). To better understand all this, I will refer to some letters that allow the reader to better analyse Tolkien's concept of 'pity'.

In draft letter n. 153 of September 1954 addressed to Peter Hastings (Tolkien, 2006c, 191), sharing observations about the fact that, according to him, the Troll Gugliemo had felt pity for Bilbo, the Professor highlighted that in every type of world – Primary or Secondary, real or imaginary – everything must submit to the Will of God: this was also true for Arda, Middle-earth and its inhabitants.

Tolkien, as sub-creator, had given powers to some of his imaginary creatures, such as the word to the Trolls. However, they did not possess what was proper, for example, of Men and Hobbits, i.e. a sentient soul capable of moral acts, including pity. Indeed, for the Professor: "Pity must restrain one from doing something immediately desirable and seemingly advantageous." (191).

That attitude would have been possible only for those who, after careful reflection and evaluation, had managed to draw an ethical judgment on the actions to be performed and their consequences.

This is the moral and imaginative value of pity: those who, like Trolls, possess neither soul nor moral capacity, nor even imagination, would never be able to feel pity for anyone. Instead, having all these characteristics, Bilbo and Frodo brought this life with Gollum.

Furthermore, in a note of the draft letter n. 246 of September 1963 addressed to Mrs. Eileen Elgar, in commenting on the events that took place at the Crack of Doom, Tolkien thus stated:

> In the sense that 'pity' to be a true virtue must be directed to the good of its object. It is empty if it is exercised *only* to keep oneself 'clean', free from hate or the actual doing of injustice, though this is also a good motive. (330)

From these words, it is evident that the Professor had a non-egoistic concept of pity in mind: instead, to be fully a virtue, a *habitus*, to show all its moral and imaginative character, it had to be *for* someone, i.e. for their good.

The repercussions for the subject who developed this virtue would have been only 'secondary' and accessory, not dependent on their will. Indeed, as will be seen in the next paragraph dedicated to Frodo, Tolkien considered the act of mercy towards a character like Gollum to be an act of madness, or of mystical faith in the supreme value-in-itself of mercy and generosity (cf. 234).

Here, then, is also the reason why the term 'Pity', in Gandalf's speech, is written with a capital letter: what mattered to Tolkien was 'Pity' as a 'supreme value-in-itself', not folded into itself or concerned with one's own personal gain, but turned and open to the salvation of the other for whom it was possible to feel "Pity" and "Mercy" (Tolkien, 2005, 59).

Furthermore, 'Mercy' is the second essential element contained in Gandalf's words to Frodo at Bag End. In short, what had blocked Bilbo in his intent to kill Gollum had not only been a moral virtue, an altruism concerned with both the safety of others and his own, but there had also been another element at play: 'Mercy'.

In Tolkien's mind, 'Pity' and 'Mercy' were not the same thing and, therefore, they did not derive from the same source. This is shown by the fact that he placed a separation between the two terms. So both of these concepts can be traced to that episode in the caves, but in a different and complementary way.

The term "Mercy" is also placed with a capital letter, to indicate, once again, that it must be understood as a 'supreme value-in-itself': that is, Mercy in its highest degree. In this respect, in the letter n. 113 of the Septuagesima 1948 addressed to C.S. Lewis – which can be considered a fundamental text for understanding the events at the Crack of Doom, even if it is not focussed on the tales of Middle-earth, but on religious and moral topics in the Primary World – thus, Tolkien stated:

> What happens when the culprit is genuinely repentant, but the sufferer is deeply resentful and withholds all 'forgiveness'? It is a terrible thought, to deter anyone from running the risk of needlessly causing such an 'evil'. Of course, the power of mercy is only delegated and is always exercised with or without cooperation by Higher Authority. But the joys and healing of cooperation must be lost? (Tolkien, 2006c, 127)

In these words, through which the concepts of 'forgiveness' and 'mercy' are united and identified with each other, it is evident that the Professor conceived the supreme Mercy, the absolute value-in-itself, in its ontological essence, not as an anthropological or moral characteristic but, conversely, as something purely and primarily 'theological', belonging to God.

Therefore, for Tolkien, the power of mercy could only be 'delegated' to a human being, but its real owner – that is, the one who actually had the power to act with or without human help – was always the Supreme Authority, the omnipotent and infinitely merciful God.

However, the acts of mercy performed by men and women would not be lost: in fact, they are capable of producing beneficial effects on both the ones who perform them and on their recipients.

This vision of Mercy is perfectly compatible with the one in the Legendarium, in Gandalf's speech to Frodo, and in the entirety of *The Lord of the Rings*.

Therefore, Gollum, despite his defects, his pettiness and malice, was the character for whom Pity and Mercy never let their presence fail. However, accepting all of this requires a profound and sincere will to change one's life, to return to living fully in the light of the sun.

The path to Mordor also helped Gollum to understand all this, allowing him, above all, to confront himself and others who, despite many doubts and uncertainties, had shown him the beauty of friendship, goodness and forgiveness.

5.2 Gollum and Frodo: a relationship of pity, mercy and forgiveness of injury

What has just been examined regarding the Pity and Mercy that occurred in the meeting between Bilbo and Gollum can also be found in the very special relationship between the Stoor and Frodo. In draft letter n. 181 of January-February 1956 addressed to Michael Straight, Tolkien, speaking of Frodo's failure, thus stated:

> But at this point the 'salvation' of the world and Frodo's own 'salvation' is achieved by his previous *pity* and forgiveness of injury. [...] To 'pity' him, to forbear to kill him, was a piece of folly, or a mystical belief in the ultimate value-in-itself of pity and generosity. (Tolkien, 2006c, 234)

Or, even more clearly, in draft letter n. 191 of 26th July 1956 written to Miss J. Burn, it is said that: "[Frodo] (and the Cause) were saved – by Mercy: by the supreme value and efficacy of Pity and forgiveness of injury" (Tolkien, 2006c, 251-252).

And finally, in letter n. 192 of 27th July 1956 addressed to Amy Ronald, Tolkien specified that:

> It is possible for the good, even the saintly, to be subjected to a power of evil which is too great for them to overcome – in themselves. In this case the cause (not the 'hero') was triumphant, because by the exercise of pity, mercy, and forgiveness of injury, a situation was produced in which all was redressed and disaster averted. (252-253)

Therefore, both the history of the world of Arda and Frodo's life had been saved by the same elements that had allowed Bilbo to escape unscathed from the caves of the Misty Mountains and Gollum to survive for the umpteenth time: i.e. 'Pity', 'Mercy' and 'forgiveness' of injury.

However, it should be noted that Frodo too had to make an existential journey to be able to get physically and emotionally close to that miserable creature who was spasmodically looking for his 'Preciousss'.

The first inclination Frodo had, as with Bilbo, was to reject Gollum, feeling a total absence of pity for him. A trace of this can be found once again in the dialogue between Gandalf and Frodo in the chapter 'The Shadow of the Past' in *The Lord of the Rings*:

> 'He deserves death.' 'Deserves it! I daresay he does. Many that live deserve death. And some that die deserve life. Can you give it to them? Then do not be too eager to deal out death in judgement. [...] I have not much hope that Gollum can be cured before he dies, but there is a chance of it. And he is bound up with the fate of the Ring. My heart tells me that

> he has some part to play yet, for good or ill, before the end; and when that comes, the pity of Bilbo may rule the fate of many – yours not least'. (Tolkien, 2005, 59)

The words of this text are relevant and represent a certain type of attitude that is still strongly present in our society today: that is, the fear of something or someone you don't know can lead directly to the absence of any kind of pity in your comparisons and to consider the other person as an enemy to be executed by transforming law, or justice, into vengeance.

Frodo, paralysed by terror at what he had 'heard' about Gollum, had fallen into a deadly trap – both for himself and that wretched creature – of prejudgment, a discriminating preunderstanding, and the emanation of a 'sentence' of conviction without appeal.

However, once again, Gandalf tried to place a different consideration in Frodo's heart. The Wizard had enticed the Hobbit into having the courage to test his preconceived ideas about Gollum, should they ever meet. In fact, the Stoor was certainly a treacherous and wicked person and, according to the common schemes of a rigid and inflexible law, he would have deserved death; but there was something else to discover. To understand this, it would be necessary for Frodo to 'see' Gollum; that is, to experience him and what he had lived.

All this leads to a statement from St. Thomas Aquinas contained in the *Summa Theologiae* – a work that Tolkien knew and possessed an ancient edition of (cf. Cilli, 2019, 287) – which explains this passage very well. Thomas, precisely speaking of the laws in a commentary on *Metaphysics* by Aristotle, wrote thus: "*Sed ratio humana non est mensura rerum, sed potius e converso*" (Thomas Aquinas, I-II, q. 91, a. 3); that is, human reason is not the parameter by which to judge things, but things allow human beings to understand if their reasoning, if everything they have imprinted in their minds, responds to truth, or else they are only false prejudices or non-existent realities.

Therefore, healthy medieval realism allows the reader to better understand the words of Gandalf, who was concerned with correcting Frodo's prejudgment and making him understand that he should not consider himself the dispenser of someone's life and death. Even the ignoble Gollum would have his last and decisive part in the fate of the Ring and in the Hobbit's life. This would result because of Bilbo's pity, Gandalf's care, and the gentleness and delicacy of the Elves' wise and good hearts.

In this circle of love and forgiveness, Frodo also played his part and changed his mind. In fact, of particular importance, is his first meeting with Gollum, as told in the chapter 'The Taming of Sméagol' in *The Lord of the Rings*.

In this, Tolkien accurately described how Frodo and Sam secretly watched and listened to Gollum, hearing his voice, his cries, his protests. They had noticed his behaviour, namely that of a sort of slimy little animal, a thin and solitary spider, a rejected and desperate Stoor, a "wretched creature" in search of its lost "Preciousss" (cf. Tolkien, 2005, 612-615).

The reaction of the two Hobbits was different: Sam attacked Gollum in order to capture and then tie him up, with the desire to leave him in those cold and dark lands; instead, Frodo, despite having drawn his sword and forced Gollum to surrender under threat of death, managed to look deeply into the Stoor.

In this meeting, many thoughts rushed into Frodo's mind, including the dialogue he'd had with Gandalf at Bag End, where the Wizard had told him: "Then do not be too eager to deal out death in judgment" (Tolkien, 2005, 59). Confronted with Gollum, in Frodo's mind, that sentence had become more like this: "Then be not too eager to deal out death in the name of justice, fearing for your own safety" (Tolkien, 2005, 615).

This difference could only appear to be an error by Tolkien who, not remembering the sentence well, had rewritten it in a different way. In reality, it is necessary to immerse oneself in the context in which these words were reworked in Frodo's soul, in thoughts which reflected his state of mind in that heightened moment.

With this modification, the Hobbit shifted his attention from what he had previously stated – in a general and theoretical way from the viewpoint of a merciless judge – to the concrete reality facing him in that moment. He realised that the death he had theoretically wanted to dish out to Gollum, he was now actually capable of inflicting in the name of justice and fear for his safety. This change from the general to the particular, from pure theory to practice, characterised by looking Gollum in the eye, sensing his miseries and torment, had radically changed Frodo's way of being and seeing things.

In fact, two elements merged in this episode, causing Frodo to take pity: first of all, like Gollum, he had worn and was carrying the Ring, the burden so heavy that it placed a strain on body and mind. Secondly, as mentioned earlier, during that moment of reflection, Frodo began to come to terms with himself, with his prejudices, with what he had thought up to then, and with what, instead, had flowed from his heart upon meeting the Stoor.

However, his fear remained, and he could not hide it even from 'someone absent' (most likely himself or Gandalf, with whom he had previously discussed Gollum). However, this fear of the unknown had been mitigated – or in any case contrasted – by the direct experience of his senses and his mind when meeting that miserable creature. Finally, Frodo could see Gollum and, as was the case also for Bilbo, Gandalf, and the Elves, felt Pity.

5.3 Gollum and Sam: from hatred to compassion

As for the relationship between Sam and Gollum, it can be seen from the passages quoted that they detested each other. They exchanged words of hatred and contempt, Sam distrusting even when Gollum seemed harmless. Indeed, they almost engaged in a scuffle near Shelob's lair.

However, it was here that something important happened: Frodo, stunned by an almost fatal blow from the great Spider, was almost captured by Orcs while Sam, after putting Shelob to flight, and now convinced of his master's death, began to fight with himself, trying to figure out what to do next.

The decision he made was to take the Ring with him and put it on his finger in order to free his master from the clutches of the Orcs. Through this gesture, Sam began to understand what it meant to be prey to the lust for that evil seal and experienced the way it subjected its bearer to a test of will and physical resistance.

This allowed him later, on the slopes of Mount Doom, both to 'see' Gollum – who he had previously only wanted to kill for the evil he had inflicted on Frodo – and to feel 'compassion' and 'pity' for him (cf. Tolkien, 2055, 944-945).

This was possible because both had 'suffered' the same pain and the same attraction for the Ring. However, Sam had managed to give it back to Frodo, while Gollum remained chained to it. Perhaps the awareness of no longer being bound by that burden and of having freely renounced it, allowed that little gardener of the Shire to feel compassion and pity for Gollum who, on the other hand, would never have been able to free himself from the spell of that powerful Ring.

5.4 Gollum and Faramir: a look at justice softened by mercy

One of the most significant passages within Tolkien's stories, which demonstrates how much Gollum was the 'ignoble wanted, chased and found by mercy', is undoubtedly his meeting with Faramir, in the chapter 'The Forbidden Pool' in *The Lord of the Rings* (cf. Tolkien, 2005, 690-693). Indeed, the Stoor had transgressed the law of Gondor whereby foreigners could not enter Henneth Annûn without formal permission.

5.4.1 Sméagol and his master: an apparent and saving deception

Before talking about this episode, it is necessary to analyse what happened in the moments preceding the direct encounter between Faramir and Gollum: that is, the harrowing scene in which Frodo, through a stratagem and an 'apparent deception' had managed to save Gollum from certain death (see Tolkien, 2005, 687-689).

In this situation, once again, Frodo had pity and mercy on Gollum. However, this happened thanks to Faramir who, in an extraordinaryly maieutic way, had questioned the Hobbit about what to do: since he was now able to 'see Gollum', it was essential that Frodo provided the reason for why that wretched creature deserved to live rather than to be killed by the archers of Gondor.

Therefore, this event can be considered as a sort of parallel tale to the first meeting between the Hobbit and the Stoor: for a second time, Frodo had the possibility of getting rid of Gollum, but the memory of Gandalf's words and the pity that he had shown to the Stoor, along with Gollum's wretched condition and the fact that this creature had now earned certain rights and credit in the presence of his Master – as a guide who had led him and Sam unharmed through the Marshes – all made Frodo's heart swell. As a result, he begged Faramir to spare Gollum and allow him to persuade the wretched creature to leave the Forbidden Pool.

But Frodo's chosen way of doing this consisted of a small lie, relying on the trust which had been granted to him by Gollum. This led to the Stoor's capture. In fact, not understanding what was happening, Gollum interpreted his Master's behaviour as a betrayal. Frodo testified in his favour, though, to prevent him from being mistreated more than necessary. However, the Hobbit felt immensely unhappy along with a sense of profound unkindness for what he had done to Gollum.

5.4.2 Gollum being judged by Faramir: between 'equity' and 'aequitas canonica'

Once captured and brought before Faramir, Gollum was put on trial. However, this was a particular kind of judgment which, in order to be understood in its entirety, must necessarily be addressed in detail.

The Captain of Gondor knew how to read the hearts of his interlocutors and to feel pity and mercy for them. This also allowed him to 'see' Gollum. Indeed, Faramir had the Stoor untied and brought before him. In the role of judge, he was 'sitting in court' with two witnesses beside him, in the form of Sam and Frodo.

Faramir looked Gollum in the eyes. In that instant, through his 'penetrating gaze', he managed to truly 'see' that miserable creature and understand his true nature. For this reason, he said: "There are locked doors and closed windows in your mind, and dark rooms behind them" (Tolkien, 2005, 689).

Faramir had managed to unhinge Gollum's defences, penetrating to the depths of his soul: he understood both his inner torment and the erosion of his heart due to the malice already present in him, taken to the extreme by the Ring – that is, he had investigated the essence of Gollum – along with the crime of murder which he had committed when he was still simply Sméagol.

However, this also led him to feel pity and to know how to discern which specific legal means was most suitable in that specific case. For this, he decided to resort to a 'process' in which justice – of which he was the bearer – was perfectly and naturally united with mercy.

Having entered Henneth Annûn uninvited to feed on the fish present in the forbidden pool, Gollum had committed a violation punishable by death. The specific term used by Tolkien is 'trespass' which, in the eyes of a canonist and a comparative jurist, immediately refers to 'writ of trespass' – or, rather, to 'trespass on the case' – which were born and developed within English medieval law.

Therefore, as an accomplished medievalist, the Professor most likely knew this particular feature of Norman English law from the Thirteenth Century. Actually, having been caught in the act of committing a crime, Gollum was accused of violating a law of Gondor – i.e. the 'trespass' – for which, the 'compensation by equivalent' was death. Obviously, such an excessive extension of the compensation served Tolkien in maintaining a sense of narrative tension and the tragic nature of the story.

Furthermore, this penalty served the task of stimulating the various characters to show pity and mercy for Gollum. This provoked Frodo's request to spare him, because the Stoor was likely unaware of having transgressed a human law.

In reality, both in the context of common law and in this account, 'trespass on the case' allowed protection for cases in which there was no wilful misconduct, but instead simple negligence.

Given that the charge has been identified, our reflection must focus on the procedure implemented in this judgment as described in Tolkien's story. One point should be kept in mind: never in a single instance did Faramir appear to have thought of Gollum as mentally ill, schizophrenic or bipolar.

This is demonstrated by the fact that, without any delay, he subjected Gollum to a criminal trial with the eventual imposition of a sentence for transgessing the law of Gondor. This shows that Tolkien was most likely aware of the fact that a person *non compos sui* – i.e. not in control of himself and his own actions, mentally unstable, or not capable of understanding – could not be subjected to trial. If he had been, he could not have been blamed and he could not be sentenced to death.

Therefore, the juridical reference to the procedure which the author was most likely inspired by in this passage from *The Lord of the Rings* was the procedure of 'equity' combined with the exercise of the '*aequitas canonica*'.

In short, the English and Catholic sources of Canon Law were combined together by Tolkien and merged in the description of the judgment against Gollum by Faramir.

Actually, as in the equity proceedings of English medieval law, Faramir, son of Denethor, his lieutenant, can be considered as a kind of royal Chancellor with judicial power, who had decided to enact justice, taking into account the circumstances of the case and not remaining rigidly bound to the general and abstract norm.

Therefore, the Professor had referred to the specifically English and Catholic cultural baggage to enrich his text with both juridical and metajuridical elements. In them, justice, piety and mercy merged.

Furthermore, in the text of the judgment against Gollum, there is a significant element that changed the fate of the trial: while, on the one hand, Faramir had urged Frodo to reflect on the reasons why Gollum deserved to be saved and not killed, on the other, the Hobbit himself had put a substantial question to the Captain of Gondor, which had caused him to reflect.

In fact, after Gollum's promise to Faramir not to return to those places and not to reveal to anyone all that he had seen, Frodo said to the Captain: "At least, you must either accept this promise or carry out your law. You will get no more" (Tolkien, 2005, 690).

In short, the Hobbit was trying to take Faramir's discussion and reasoning beyond the cold and sterile application of the *littera legis* to arrive at a different or, at least broader, judgment that took into account all the circumstances.

Indeed, this happened: Faramir, Captain of Gondor, conscience of the Steward, a just but also merciful judge, on the one hand exacted justice by condemning Gollum – as a transgressor of a pre-established law – but, on the other, managed to mitigate this decision, entrusting the creature into the hands of Frodo, who had previously been deemed innocent and free to travel to those places.

Furthermore, in order to make this sentence perpetual, it had to be validated after one year before Denethor. Therefore, Faramir understood Frodo's mission and his words regarding Gollum, his guide to whom he owed his life, along with a promise of protection and custody. He had applied what in today's and medieval Canon Law is defined as '*aequitas canonica*'.

This was a legal institution that Tolkien was most likely familiar with through the works of the Italian cardinal and medieval canonist, Enrico da Susa, known as the Ostiensis. In England, he was known because he lived there between the '30s and '40s of the Twenty-Third Century and held some diplomatic posts in the service of the King of England until 1258.

Within Canon law, the Ostiensis is known for having given an extraordinarily precise description of the *aequitas canonica*. In the *Summa aurea* – probably composed in 1239 – he had written: "*Aequitas est iustitia dulcore misericordiae temperata*" (Enrico da Susa, 1537, fol. 289rb).

For this reason, Faramir – as a good judge – had used the legal instruments available to him to affirm the reasons for the law. However, he had not let himself be overwhelmed by the rigidity of its norms: when given the opportunity, he managed to 'see' Gollum by looking him in the eyes and had reflected on his miserable condition and how his existence was inextricably linked to the Frodo's mission. Therefore, he had not been able to do anything but feel pity and compassion for Gollum and placed on him 'a gaze of justice softened by mercy'.

6. The events at the Crack of Doom

The path taken so far was aimed at arriving at the final events of *The Lord of the Rings*, in which it is told of the annihilation of the Ring of Power and Gollum's death in the blazing fires of the Crack of Doom.

In several letters, Tolkien spoke about the narrative construction of this episode. For example, in draft letter n. 181 of January-February 1956 addressed to Michael Straight, he stated:

> The 'catastrophe' *exemplifies* (an aspect of) the familiar words: 'Forgive us our trespasses as we forgive them that trespass against us. Lead us not into temptation, but deliver us from evil.' [...] The view, in the term of my story, is that though every event or situation has (at least) two aspects: the history and development of the individual [...], and the history of the world (which depends on his action for its own sake). (Tolkien, 2006c, 233)

Therefore, the final scene set on Mount Doom was constructed by Tolkien as the nodal and essential point in which all the narrative threads of the story, intertwining, would compose a tapestry of extraordinary beauty. Indeed, in it, the fates of Frodo, Sam and Gollum are fulfilled but, at the same time, also the inhabitants of Middle-earth, of the One Ring and the Ring-maker, Sauron, the Dark Lord of Mordor and his faithful Nazgûl.

The individual doom of the characters in action, combined with that of all the Arda, had brought about the end of the Third Age, thus giving rise to the Dominion of Men. After these events, some of the last Elves and Istari left for the Blessed Realm: Galadriel, Elrond, and Gandalf left Middle-earth to return to the true West.

The known story until then ended but the events of Crack of Doom had shown 'how' and 'why' all that had happened. So, let's follow in the footsteps of the two Hobbits and Gollum to try to actually understand what Tolkien wanted to communicate and narrate in the final scenes of *The Lord of the Ring*.

6.1 Frodo's failure and Mount Doom: between 'catastrophe', 'eucatastrophe' and 'dyscatastrophe'

Now, it is important to speak about 'Frodo's failure' and his 'sacrificial situation'. It must be kept in mind that his failure was necessary from a narrative point of view as it represented what, in the essay "On Fairy-stories", the Professor called a 'dyscatastrophe', i.e. "the existence […] of sorrow and failure" (Tolkien, 2006b, 153).

Frodo had experienced both of these pains. In fact, once back in the Shire, he no longer felt part of that world. The Hobbit was almost like a veteran returned from battle, a misfit in the throes of physical pain due to wounds sustained during the War of the Ring and moral suffering for his 'failure', for having given way in the moment he tried to 'prove' himself, for not having been able to resist the temptation to put the Ring on his finger instead of throwing it into the fires of Mount Doom.

However, all this was necessary for the 'dyscatastrophe' to be fulfilled narratively. The latter also allowed Frodo to experience another very acute pain: that of the fleeting vision of Joy which, albeit through a physical mutilation, had poured the beneficial consequences of the 'eucatastrophe' on him.

At this point, it is important to understand the essential content of both dyscatastrophe and eucatastrophe, starting from the central nucleus of these two words: that is, the 'catastrophe'.

Tolkien himself brought back the meaning and sense of the 'catastrophe' in his stories. In fact, in the aforementioned draft letter n. 181, he stated:

> I should say that within the mode of the story the 'catastrophe' *exemplifies* (an aspect of) the familiar words: 'Forgive us our trespasses as we forgive them that trespass against us. Lead us not into temptation, but deliver us from evil.' (Tolkien, 2006c, 233)

This means that the 'dyscatastrophe' is to be considered as the non-fulfilment of this evangelical invocation, while the 'eucatastrophe' is the full and sudden realisation of the words of the Lord's Prayer – Our Father.

The exemplification consists in reporting narratively, as an example in the Secondary World, a general principle of the Primary World, without however resulting in allegory or applicability. In this case, the general principle is purely theological in nature. Therefore, being an invocation addressed to the Divinity, it is essential that God in the primary story and Eru in the secondary narrative are the subjects appointed to respond to the content of this request through its realisation or its failure.

Indeed, in two letters, the Professor stated exactly this. In the first place, in draft letter n. 191 of 26th July 1956 addressed to Miss J. Burn, it is written: "No, Frodo 'failed'. [...] The power of Evil in the world is *not* finally resistible by incarnate creatures, however 'good'; and the Writer of the Story is not one of us" (Tolkien, 2006c, 252).

And in the following letter n. 192 of 27th July 1956 addressed to Amy Ronald, it is stated:

> Frodo deserved all honour because he spent every drop of his power of will and body, and that was just sufficient to bring him to the destined point, and no further. Few others, possibly no others of his time, would have got so far. The Other Power then took over: the Writer of the Story (by which I do not mean myself), 'that one ever-present Person who is never absent and never named' [*Actually referred to as 'the One' in App. A III p. 317 l. 20. The Númenóreans (and Elves) were absolute monotheists]. (253)

Consequently, in Tolkien's mind and in the plot of his story, the ending of *The Lord of the Rings* must necessarily be 'theocentric' or, as he himself said in the essay "On Fairy-stories", 'Mystical'. Indeed:

> Something really 'higher' is occasionally glimpsed in mythology: Divinity, the right to power (as distinct from its possession), the due of worship: in fact 'religion'. […] Even fairy-stories as a whole have three faces: the Mystical towards the Supernatural; the Magical towards Nature; and the Mirror of scorn and pity towards Man. The essential face of Faërie is the middle one, the Magical. But the degree in which the others appear (if at all) is variable, and may be decided by the individual story-teller. (Tolkien, 2006b, 124-125)

Also, Tolkien, as narrator, decided that the Face of the Mirror of scorn and pity towards Man should have turned several times, especially towards Gollum, the ignoble 'sought', 'pursued' and 'found' by Pity and Mercy.

While the Mystical Face focussed more on the basic conflict with Sauron and the destruction of the Ring of Power, in fact, in letter n. 183 of 1956, containing some notes regarding W.H. Auden's review of *The Return of the King*, it is written that: "In *The Lord of the Rings* the conflict is not basically about 'freedom', though that is naturally involved. It is about God, and His sole right to divine honour" (Tolkien, 2006c, 243).

In a certain way, in this respect, Tolkien's story brought with it a narrative reflection that could almost be defined as a *De vera religione* of Middle-earth, even if Eru, i.e. God, is never named but is, at the same time, 'that one ever-present Person who is never absent'.

Taking all this into account, it seems justifiable that the assertion according to which, narratively and conceptually speaking, the ending of *The Lord of the Rings* – in relation to the events at the Crack of Doom – was necessarily constructed by Tolkien in a 'theocentric' or 'Mystical' way.

Indeed, only God could have demonstrated His exclusive right to divine honour as opposed to the Satanic cult of Melkor and the evil Lordship of Sauron. This He had accomplished in the past – but most noticeably – before the end of the Second Age of Middle-earth.

'The Fall of Númenor' and 'The Fall of The Lord of the Rings' are inextricably linked, mainly due to the central role of God in both events. This presence and action of the Divinity was performed explicitly in the first case and implicitly in the second.

6.2 Mount Doom and the 'Deus absconditus'

One of the most important narrative problems that Tolkien probably had to face was finding a way to present the 'theocentric' or 'Mystical' aspects at the end of *The Lord of the Rings* without an explicit reference to God, but with an interaction between Eru, the '*Deus absconditus*', and the story of Frodo and the Ring.

What could be the most eloquent sign – that it could speak with Men's words but at the same time recount Eru's intervention in Middle-earth – of the supernatural presence at Mount Doom? It is very likely that, to indicate 'theophany', Tolkien used a narrative device already present in Holy Scriptures: that is, the description of a fiery and erupting mountain that causes earthquakes, roars and swirls in the air. (Ex19:16-19).

On closer inspection, this was the same situation as Mount Doom and the surrounding areas both before the Ring was claimed and worn by Frodo and, more importantly, when it fell into the fire. To this theophany a second element must be added: the name of the Mount.

In Tolkien's works, the word 'doom' is used in its most diverse meanings: 'fate', 'destiny', 'sentence', 'judgment', 'disaster', etc. One of the major equivalences that the Professor used was between 'doom' and 'impending fate'.

This probably allows the reader to connect what is contained in the ending of *The Lord of the Rings* with the whole Anglo-Saxon tradition about the '*metodsceaft*'. This term expresses a sense of disaster and death. Actually, at Mount Doom, there were: Gollum's death, the destruction of the One Ring, the Fall of Sauron and the collapse of his fortress in Mordor.

This 'impending fate' had been 'foretold' in ancient and mysterious prophecies relayed to Imladris during the Council of Elrond. In that meeting, Boromir talked of a prophecy that appeared in a dream both to him and even earlier to his brother Faramir (Tolkien, 2005, 246).

The relationship between the events at Mount Doom and these dreams allows the perception that behind this impending fate there was something else: a larger reality at work, driving the events of Middle-earth. Basically, what the screaming voice in the dreams was prophesying was nothing to do with the doom of Minas Tirith but, rather, to announce that the 'Doom', the 'Judgment', which could not be emitted by anyone summoned to the Council of Elrond, was imminent, as the Sword of Elendil had been rebuilt and the Ring found. In short, the 'Day of Judgment' had now come.

From all this, the connection between the 'Doom' (i.e. the 'Judgment', the final end of the Third Age) and 'Mount Doom' (conceived as the place and time of the 'impending fate') is clearer. The possibility of glimpsing this supernatural dimension or, as Tolkien would say, 'Mystical', is also provided in the place where all this happened in the story: the Crack of Doom.

On the one hand, in the Christian tradition, it is indicated by the sound of the last trumpet while, on the other hand, in Tolkien's tales, it is the crack in the Orodruin crater into which the Ring of Power was thrown (Tolkien, 1975). Therefore, this physical rift in the Mount allowed the Hobbits to become aware of the dimension where the Judgment of Eru had been passed on Sauron and the entire Third Age of Middle-earth.

One wonders, however, why Tolkien wanted to insert these concepts and aspects within the final part of his literary work. The answer is possibly found in the essay "On Fairy-stories", in which the Professor spoke about an anecdote that happened to another great English writer whom he had known well since his adolescence, G.K. Chesterton.

In this episode, Chesterton underlined the importance of the Day of Judgment at the end of a fairy-tale in which justice triumphs (Tolkien, 2006b, 136-137). As a result, Tolkien wanted to insert the Last Judgment into the final part of *The Lord of the Rings*, that is, the 'theocentric' and 'Mystical' part, in which Justice and Mercy were fully and evidently manifested.

Actually, in the events of Bilbo, Frodo and the other exceptional Hobbits, and especially in this final part of the stories of the Third Age of Middle-earth, the Professor was able to deploy all the narrative force of:

> a. what he had found written in *Beowulf*, that the manifested truth is that mighty God has ruled the race of men through all the ages (cf. Tolkien, 2019, 70);
> b. what he noted in the critical essay *Beowulf: the Monsters*

and the Critics, where God is conceived as the arbiter of critical events and the *Metod* (cf. Tolkien, 2006a, 40);
c. what he had specified in the explanatory note contained in the essay on *Beowulf* about the fact that, in Old English, '*Metod*' is the word that is most nearly allied to 'fate', although employed as a synonym of God (cf. Tolkien, 2006b, 47).

Therefore, all of Tolkien's philological-literary reflections on the concept of '*Metod*' and '*wyrd*', in *Beowulf* and in other northern European cultures, allowed him to make Eru present, in a narrative way, in the events at Mount Doom.

Although never mentioned, Eru is present in every page of *The Lord of the Rings*, and especially in the events at the Crack of Doom. This is more understandable if I refer to what Tolkien wrote in the "Guide to Names" about the fact how Mount Doom was the equivalent in the common language of Gondor for the Elvish '*Amon Amarth*'.

If one looks at the essay *Fate and Free Will*, they can realise that the root of the word '*Amarth*' is 'MBAR', which means to settle in a place, to establish one's home, to erect permanent buildings, to dwell (cf. Tolkien, 2009, 184). From this, it can be deduced how '*Amarth*' carries with it both the sense of something 'fixed' (such as Fate and Destiny) as well as the act of building a house or inhabiting a place.

This second meaning allows the reader to understand how much the category of theophany can act as one of the keys to reading the events at Mount Doom. Actually, while The One did not physically reside anywhere in Arda, during what occurred at the Crack of Doom in the Third Age of Middle-earth, 'the Authority that ordained the Rules', 'The Other Power', Eru, temporarily established His abode in

Mount Doom, in the place where every other power had been overwhelmed, including the Phial of Galadriel.

This allowed God to take control of the situation after Frodo's failure (i.e. the dyscatastrophe), when all seemed lost and, thanks also to Gollum's intervention, put an end to the existence of the Ring and the Power of Sauron.

This last scene represents the eucatastrophe in Tolkien's tale, in which philology and literature, Providence and Fate have united and have given full realisation to the general principle exemplified in the story and underlying all these events, namely the final part of the prayer, Our Father: "Forgive us our trespasses as we forgive them that trespass against us. Lead us not into temptation, but deliver us from evil".

This allowed Tolkien to show how divine honour is due only to God in Arda and that, although Middle-earth may appear, at first glance, as a world in which the supernatural seems to be non-existent, in reality, Eru was present and acted with a powerful hand both to guide and defend the humble and simple Hobbits, who had freely accepted their journey, and to show the several faces of God's infinite mercy to an ignoble creature like Gollum.

6.3 "Nine-Fingered Frodo": the meaning of being 'incomplete'

Within Tolkien's works, both in *The Lord of the Rings* and in his *Legendarium*, many of the protagonists are 'delimbed'. This physical and existential condition has been described by the Professor in different ways within the events of the characters in his stories.

If, for Beren and Frodo, being injured and without a limb constituted their 'salvation', the positive conclusion of a mission that had seemed lost, for Sauron, however, Isildur cutting off his finger represented one of his greatest defeats.

In fact, those who trusted in wickedness and power wanted to be 'complete', 'totipotent' and 'omnipotent'. Meanwhile, those who had remained 'humble', knowing that they were limited, had managed to accept their failure, in the belief that they had carried out their role with strength and dignity and had let themselves be guided by something or someone who would then complete the Quest.

Taking this into account, Frodo's loss of a limb had a very particular meaning which is connected in a decisive way to what was said in the previous paragraphs on the final events of the life of the Ring. First of all, it is worth quoting a passage from the chapter 'The Field of Cormallen' in *The Return of the King*, which recounts what happened to Frodo and Sam immediately after they emerged from the Crack of Doom:

> They stood now; and Sam still holding his master's hand caressed it. He sighed. 'What a tale we have been in, Mr. Frodo, haven't we?' he said. 'I wish I could hear it told! Do you think they'll say: *Now comes the story of Nine-fingered Frodo and the Ring of Doom?* And then everyone will hush, like we did, when in Rivendell they told us the tale of Beren One-hand and the Great Jewel. I wish I could hear it! And I wonder how it will go on after our part.' (Tolkien, 2005, 950)

So, in this passage Sam, making explicit reference to Beren One-hand and wondering how the story would continue after them, had implicitly taken up the speech he had made on the Stairs of Cirith Ungol, according to which stories and great tales have no end.

Frodo became "Nine-fingered", but not as a punishment for his failure. Instead, such a condition was proof of God's closeness, and his Providence, in the life of this little Hobbit of the Shire, and his induction into the glory of the great 'delimbed', 'imperfect' and 'incomplete' heroes.

In fact, Tolkien stated that the honour bestowed on Frodo and Sam had been rightly paid precisely because they had not altered the events: the loss of Frodo's finger and the telling of the story in its fullness and truth allowed Frodo a state of humility and, at the same time, of being saved, sanctified and praised. This was not because he had succumbed to temptation – in an almost unChristian titanic and voluntary effort – but despite his failure.

For this, the Hobbit would be remembered in stories as "Nine-Fingered Frodo". However, it is necessary to investigate which of Frodo's fingers was bitten off. This may seem like a minor detail but, in terms of narrative and the values it expresses, in my opinion, it carries fundamental importance.

In the stories of *The Hobbit* and *The Lord of the Rings*, it is often indicated that Bilbo or Frodo put the Ring on a generic finger while, in some particular cases, it is specified that this finger was the "index of the left hand" (cf. Tolkien, 2011, 78; Tolkien, 2005, 195). Instead, in Tom Bombadil's case, it was the "little finger" of an unspecified hand (cf. Tolkien, 2005, 133).

Finally, with regards to the finger which Frodo put the Ring on at the moment of him laying claim to it at the Crack of Doom, the text does not immediately identify it, but it can be understood through a passage taken from the chapter 'The Field of Cormallen' in *The Return of the King*, when the awakening of the two Hobbits is described after being rescued by eagles. It is written as follows:

> "[Sam] sat up and then he saw that Frodo was lying beside him, and slept peacefully, one hand behind his head, and the other resting upon the coverlet. It was the right hand, and the third finger was missing." (951)

Therefore, Frodo had slipped the Ring onto the third finger of the hand he was resting on the coverlet, i.e. the third finger of the right hand. As Christopher Tolkien stated in a note contained in "Sauron Defeated", in the ninth volume of *The History of Middle-earth*: "My father named the penultimate finger (the 'fourth finger' or 'ring finger') the 'third finger'; so Frodo's 'third finger was missing' (*RK,* 229)" (in Tolkien, 2017b, 51, note 9). So we can see that Gollum bit off Frodo's 'ring finger', on his right hand (see also Toninelli, 2023, 33-34).

Because of this indication, it could open a window onto a hypothesis also made by Tom Shippey (see Shippey, 2005, 164). It is probable that the Professor drew inspiration from an evangelical passage, later exemplified in the scene where Gollum bites Frodo's finger. This text is found in three similar but different versions: two in the Gospel of Matthew and one in the Gospel of Mark. Choosing purely as an example the version from the evangelist Matthew in the King James Bible (the same quoted by Shippey), it is written:

> Ye have heard that it was said by them of old time, Thou shalt not commit adultery: But I say unto you, That whosoever looketh on a woman to lust after her hath committed adultery with her already in his heart. And if thy right eye offends thee, pluck it out, and cast *it* from thee: for it is profitable for thee that one of thy members should perish, and not *that* thy whole body should be cast into hell. And if thy right hand offends

thee, cut it off, and cast *it* from thee: for it is profitable for thee that one of thy members should perish, and not *that* thy whole body should be cast into hell. (Matt 5:27-30)

As is possible to observe, the text refers to the 'right hand' and speaks about the fact that if it, or some other limb, is the cause of offence, an occasion of sin or a cause of stumbling, it should be cut off and thrown away in order to obtain life rather than be cast into hell with all limbs intact.

However, there is a substantial difference between the Gospel passages and the Crack of Doom episode: in the Gospels, the one who would have had the task of cutting off the limb for his salvation was precisely the subject himself who, realising the cause of the sin and offence, would have had to remove a part of his body at its root.

Instead, in the *The Lord of the Rings*, Frodo failed in this enterprise. In this case, once again, the theocentrism of the final scene of this story is shown: as stated by Tolkien himself, grace led to the amputation of Frodo's finger by means of Gollum, i.e. it was a gift both sudden and unexpected, permitted and willed by Eru.

In fact, describing the condition of Frodo and Sam immediately after the events at the Crack of Doom, the narrator states: "The burden was gone. His master had been saved; he was himself again, he was free" (Tolkien, 2005, 947). The words "His master had been saved" suggests that someone else had saved Frodo from the Ring and from its power. At this point, three levels of interpretation are possible:

a) *Immediate level*: it was Gollum who saved Frodo by biting his finger off;

b) *Proximate level*: it was Mercy and Pity shown by Frodo – and by other protagonists of the story – towards Gollum that allowed the Stoor to still want the Ring and to be present there, at the right moment, to snatch it from the hands of the Hobbit;

c) *Remote level*: it was Eru who moved all of the good protagonists who had met Gollum to Mercy and Pity, so that he could convert him and if, as happened, he chose to persevere in wickedness, he would still be in a position to be present at the Crack of Doom at the moment where Frodo, having succumbed to the temptation of the Ring, needed the acts of goodness that he had performed towards that miserable creature returned to him as 'grace' and, therefore, as 'salvation and sanctification'.

6.4 Gollum and the events at the Crack of Doom

If Frodo partook in the final eucatastrophe at the Crack of Doom, Gollum was certainly its main participant: his contribution fulfilled, even beyond his will, the second part of the concept of 'catastrophe', which exemplified the last sentence from Our Father; that is, to "deliver us from evil".

Certainly, that final 'grace', having saved Frodo from 'his evil', from the finger that bore the Ring, had already been a beautiful and positive consequence of a eucatastrophic event. But there was still the Quest to complete. In this sense, Gollum was an instrument of Eru and of His Providence, realising what St. Paul wrote in his First Letter to the Corinthians. Paul may have been another source of inspiration for Tolkien and, in some respects, Gollum can be considered an example of this type of divine instrument. In this letter, it is written: "God chose the lowly and despised of the world, those who count for nothing, to reduce to nothing those who are something, so that no human being might boast before God" (1Co 1:29).

Here, then, to give concreteness and realisation to the eucatastrophe in the final act, the choice fell to Gollum, 'the ignoble sought, pursued and found by Pity and Mercy'. It was not this creature who threw the Ring into the fire, but everything was accomplished 'through him' and also 'thanks to him'.

In the Latin version of Our Father, the term '*malum*' can be understood not only as a neutral (evil) but also as a masculine accusative (i.e. the Devil). Thus, through Gollum, who was despised, ignoble, and regarded as nothing to the world, the Ring of Power had been brought to nothing – it had been nullified and annihilated – and Sauron, the Dark Lord of Mordor, had been utterly defeated.

However, one question must be asked about Gollum's knowledge and awareness of all that would happen to him and the Ring at Mount Doom. In short, one wonders if he had the perfect perception of the dangers, risks and consequences of his own actions and those of others, and if he embraced all of this freely and consciously. It is important to remember again that, although corrupted and influenced by the Ring, Gollum retained his intellectual, volitional and discerning capacities.

That creature, now on the slopes of the Mountain of Fire, was perfectly aware of what was happening. It is likely that at the beginning he had only guessed what Frodo would do at Mount Doom but, subsequently, he confirmed it through a vision that the reader sees through Sam's eyes which foretells the Stoor's death.

In fact, in the chapter 'Mount Doom' in *The Return of the King*, Gollum heard that: "If you touch me ever again, you shall be cast yourself into the Fire of Doom" (Tolkien, 2005, 944). It is not possible to understand from the text if the voice was that of the Ring, or of Frodo solicited by the Ring, or of someone else, but it is only said that it emerged from the fire of the wheel that the human figure dressed in white had emblazoned on his chest.

It should be noted that, once again, the narrator used a passive voice, whereby Gollum would not have voluntarily thrown himself but he 'would have been cast' into the fire of Mount Doom. This recalls the passive form used for Frodo who, also, 'had been saved' by something or someone else.

Therefore, since the eucatastrophe can be considered as a 'single event made up of two faces' – the personal one of the protagonists and that of the general Quest – it can be said that something or someone had contextually saved Frodo and allowed Gollum to fall into the fire at the Crack of Doom.

Furthermore, the sense of abandonment that the Stoor was suffering from, touched him so deeply that, despite Sam threatening him with a sword, he did not back down but rather began to beg for mercy, stating that his will and desire was to die with his 'Precious'. Indeed, he said: "Lost lost! We're lost. And when Precious goes we'll die, yes, die into the dust" (Tolkien, 2005, 944). In short, Gollum understood that there was nothing left to do; his only choice was to pursue until the end the reconquest of his 'Precious', even if this involved his death and the destruction of the Ring.

Through this story, once again, the Professor showed that he was a 'writer of freedom of choice': until the end, Gollum pursued what was dear and important to him, regardless of the wicked essence of the heavy burden which he was giving his life for. However, this did not prevent the goodness of Frodo and humanity from being realised because of the actions and the evil will of one of the participants in the game.

This emergence of good from evil had not been an act of Gollum's will, though: he only wanted the Ring, nothing more; he wanted to be reunited with it and to die embraced by it. In fact, at the Crack of Doom, once he was holding his 'Precious' in his hands, gloating with joy and happiness, falling into the fire, the only words he managed were, "My Preciousss" (cf. 946).

But Eru, the other power at work, always present though never visible, had drawn salvation from wickedness and ennobled and sanctified the ignoble even beyond his intentions, for the good of the common Quest. At the beginning of the story of Arda in the *Music of the Ainur*, Ilúvatar had announced to Melkor that He, as God, could bring good from even the most evil deeds.

This is what happened at the Crack of Doom: Gollum put his foot in the trap and fell into the fire, as prophesied by the voice, allowing the Ring to be annihilated and Sauron to be defeated. Eru, through the ignoble, had accomplished the Quest started a long time before by a small Shire of Middle-earth, demonstrating that the right of adoration and divine honour could and should be attributed only to Him, to God.

6.5 The last forgiveness for Gollum

However, Gollum's death in the fire of Mount Doom was not the last word on him. In fact, in the final paragraph of the chapter 'Mount Doom' in *The Return of the King*, there is a dialogue between Frodo and Sam once they have escaped from the Crack of Doom. In it Frodo says: "So let us forgive him!" (947).

Therefore, Gollum had been clothed in pity even after his death: with this invocation of forgiveness, Frodo had also wanted to move Sam to compassion. In my opinion, this paragraph exemplifies two things: on the one hand, there is a quotation from something that happened to Chesterton, as reported in the essay "On Fairy-stories", according to which, at the end of the stories, children want justice because they are innocent while, instead, adults prefer forgiveness (cf. Tolkien 2006b, 136-137); on the other hand, there is a principle expressed by the Professor in letter n. 113 addressed to his friend C.S. Lewis in Septuagesima 1948. It reads as follows:

> If a man has stolen something from me, then before God I declare it a gift. [...] For it seems to me probable that such a gift has effect on the culprit's situation before God, and in any case in any true desire to 'forgive' the desire that that should be so must be present. It would be wonderful when summoned to judgement, to answer innumerable charges of wrongdoing to one's brethren, to find unexpectedly that many were not going to be preferred at all! [...] An eternal interaction of relief and gratitude. (But the culprit must be sorry). (Tolkien 2006c, 127)

So, once again Tolkien's Catholic faith led him to exemplify the principles of forgiveness and mercy in his stories towards a miserable creature called Gollum. In this 'theocentric' and 'Mystical' ending, Frodo had forgiven all of the Stoor's sins.

In fact, even the final act which mutilated him was interpreted by him as a 'gift', thanks to which the Quest had been accomplished.

For this reason, that action could be credited to Gollum as a merit where the old Stoor – now dead and freed from the serial and unnatural longevity due to the Ring – could finally be open to true immortality beyond the circles of the world, if he was arraigned and repented of his innumerable evil and mean deeds.

Therefore, the communion between Frodo and Gollum was still alive even after death, in an exchange of 'relief and gratitude'. This was a fitting conclusion for the extraordinary journey that they shared through the forests, plains and mountains of Middle-earth.

7. *Post scriptum*: a hypothetical and alternative ending for Gollum

Since great stories never finish, endings also don't end with the last page of a book. Fantasizing about what could have happened if Sam, waking up at the gates of Shelob's Lair, hadn't turned rudely towards Gollum thus allowing his repentance and his conversion and if he had welcomed him as his ancient ancestor and a Hobbit like him, Tolkien, in draft letter n. 246 of September 1963 addressed to Mrs. Eileen Elgar, imagined a hypothetical and alternative ending to the story:

> The interest would have shifted to Gollum, I think, and the battle that would have gone on between his repentance and his new love on one side and the Ring. [...] I think he would then have sacrificed himself for Frodo's sake and have *voluntarily*

cast himself into the fiery abyss. I think that an effect of his partial regeneration by love would have been a clearer vision when he claimed the Ring. [...] The only way to keep it and hurt Sauron was to destroy it and himself together – [...] this would also be the greatest service to Frodo. (Tolkien, 2006c, 330)

Therefore, this hypothetical and alternative ending would have brought the narrative back to the red thread connecting all the events up to then – i.e. the purely Hobbit-centric one – and, indeed, would have resulted in a Gollum-centric horizon: the attention would have shifted to him and his inner tension between love for Frodo and the desire to possess the Ring.

Frodo would have almost certainly been mutilated anyway, but the fate of the 'Precious' would have been entirely in Gollum's hands: he, increasingly transformed by his friendship with the Hobbit, resocialised and once more become a Stoor, would have managed to open his eyes to Sauron's evil essence and his powerlessness to counter it.

In this case, Gollum, the true protagonist of this alternative ending, would have consciously made the decision to 'voluntarily' throw himself into the fiery jaws of Mount Doom in an extreme gesture of affection for his friend Frodo. By sacrificing himself and taking the Ring with him, Gollum would have annihilated that evil object and its maker: Sauron, the Dark Lord of Mordor.

This alternative ending lets the reader see this miserable creature in a tragic and, at the same time, salvific and redemptive light, first of all for Frodo and, consequently, for all Middle-earth. Gollum, if he had consciously and voluntarily chosen to sacrifice himself for friendship, thus definitively marking his end and that of his 'Precious', would have shown once again that nothing is ever lost, that the curse could turn into a blessing for himself and for the World, and that salvation can also pass through an act of will and sacrifice from an ignoble creature now redeemed by a look of love and friendship.

Conclusion

Gollum and the ethics of the time of Mercy

My journey began with a question that arose while leafing through a booklet on *Christ and the solitude of God and of human beings* (Sassanelli, 2018) and with a reflection on a small but great sentence spoken by Jesus in the Gospel of Luke: "For where your treasure is, there also will your heart be" (Lk 12:34). From there was born the desire to travel a part of the way together with an elderly Professor of Oxford through the streets and paths of the Middle-earth that he had so well imagined and sub-created.

The thousand facets of that polyhedron that was Tolkien's life and imagination led the reader towards unimaginable horizons of linguistic reflection, literary creation, religious mysticism, evangelical proclamation, and Catholic faith. However, the central point has always been the human person and the singularity of every real or imaginary individual, man or woman, friend or adversary, with respect for differences but with awareness of the uniqueness of each one's dignity.

In the footsteps of this giant of literature of the Twentieth Century, I have managed to see beyond the ideological barriers and the great war tragedies of the last century, arriving at reflections that have touched the heart of human beings of all times and places.

Forgiveness, love, mercy, pity, chivalrous ardour, recognition of one's limits, openness towards the different, inner discernment, free will, strength of will, trusting abandonment to a greater plan, acceptance of one's mission, respect for others, pursuit of true immortality, struggle against the forces of evil inside and outside of oneself, *joie de vivre*, humility, smiles, friendship, and so on.

These are just some of the values presented by Tolkien to his readers. In fact, he has built a world that is not idyllic but a universe in which: evil really exists and often presents itself personified; memory and remembrance can become a tomb in which to embalm one's own life; power risks awakening the lowest instincts of domination towards things, nature and people; serial longevity can become such an absolute value that it must be pursued at all costs, even running the risk of bending, through technique and magic, the laws of nature, thus perverting living beings and making them become only ruthless monsters.

It is precisely one of these 'monsters' the centre of my reflection. Walking next to Sméagol-Gollum, I was able to enter the heart of Tolkien's stories as, paradoxically, this character, who exemplified the sentence from the Gospel of Luke above mentioned – the core of *The Hobbit* – and, subsequently, further embodied the characteristic essentials of *The Lord of the Rings*. From this last point of view, the gospel underlying the story of Gollum is also, together with other elements, the message at the foundation of Tolkien's entire work.

Therefore, precisely because Gollum was the 'nothing for the world' chosen to make things that are nothing and, at the same time, 'the ignoble sought, pursued and found by Pity and Mercy', it can be said that the 'Gospel of Gollum' can be defined as the 'Gospel of Mercy', in which goodness, love and forgiveness precede and exceed one's own will.

The human story of this miserable creature is made up of pettiness, wickedness, repentance that lasted for the time of a caress, openness to a friendship proposed and never imposed, but at the same time closed in on himself, desiring for a relationship but afraid to go out and discover.

Through all this, Tolkien not only addressed 'the reader' but also, above all, spoke 'about the reader'. In his works, the Professor plumbed the lowest depths of human beings, searching for that visible light even in the darkest darkness, capable of reviving what everyone believed to be dead or irrecoverable.

The undisputed queen of this inner journey of Gollum is undoubtedly 'Mercy'. Tolkien educated the reader to walk together with it, to know it and frequent it, to not be afraid of it, to be able to associate it also with the law, understanding that justice and mercy are not in opposition but, on the contrary, one can cause the softening of the other (cf. Paul VI, 2016, 7).

Tolkien gave to the Twentieth Century – a short age devastated by wars and dictatorships – a story that calls into question the responsibility of every reader, of every person who wants to build a better future.

Also referring to the great myths of the past but redesigned in the light of his Catholic faith and contemporary literary sensibility, he did not escape into a mythical past considered lost and to be viewed with nostalgia. Tolkien did not close himself in tradition but, on the contrary, presented his readers with a world of new meaning, centred on an ancient and modern pivot at the same time: Mercy.

This, like many other elements, brings Tolkien closer to Pope Francis who, at the end of the Extraordinary Jubilee of

Mercy, in the Apostolic Letter *Misericordia et misera* of 2016, thus affirmed in nos. 16 and 20-21:

> 16. Mercy *renews and redeems* because it is the meeting of two hearts: the heart of God who comes to meet the human heart. The latter is warmed and healed by the former. Our hearts of stone become hearts of flesh (cf. Ezek 36:26) capable of love despite our sinfulness. I come to realize that I am truly a "new creation" (Gal 6:15): I am loved, therefore I exist; I am forgiven, therefore I am reborn; I have been shown mercy, therefore I have become a vessel of mercy.
>
> 20. We are called to promote *a culture of mercy* based on the rediscovery of encounter with others, a culture in which no one looks at another with indifference or turns away from the suffering of our brothers and sisters. *The works of mercy are "handcrafted"*, in the sense that none of them is alike. Our hands can craft them in a thousand different ways, and even though the one God inspires them, and they are all fashioned from the same "material", mercy itself, each one takes on a different form. The works of mercy affect a person's entire life. For this reason, we can set in motion a real cultural revolution, beginning with simple gestures capable of reaching body and spirit, people's very lives.
>
> 21. *This is the time of mercy*. Each day of our journey is marked by God's presence. He guides our steps with the power of the grace that the Spirit pours into our hearts to make them capable of loving. *It is the time of mercy* for each and all, since no one can think that he or she is cut off from God's closeness and the power of his tender love. *It is the time of mercy* because those who are weak and vulnerable, distant and alone, ought to feel the presence of brothers and sisters who can help them

in their need. *It is the time of mercy* because the poor should feel that they are regarded with respect and concern by others who have overcome indifference and discovered what is essential in life. *It is the time of mercy* because no sinner can ever tire of asking forgiveness and all can feel the welcoming embrace of the Father. (Francis, 2016, 1323; 1325-1327).

In 1955, by publishing the last part of *The Lord of the Rings*, which by Tolkien's own admission is a book "that breathes Mercy from start to finish" (cf. Shippey, 2005), the Professor showed how a little Hobbit of the Shire managed to carry out daily gestures of mercy and goodness even towards a miserable and evil creature like Gollum: that actions were the cause of the salvation of Frodo and of the entire Middle-earth.

In short, unknowingly and in a literary way, Tolkien initiated that 'culture of mercy' which Pope Francis, sixty years after the publication of that Tolkienian story, indicated as a necessary attitude for the true and authentic development of human beings in the contemporary primary world.

This bridge of literature and faith, mercy and forgiveness, storytelling and real life, allows the reader to consider Mercy as the only guarantee of a better future. Only if, mindful of the past, human beings place Mercy as the essential element of present daily life, will it have the power to push every man and woman, believer and non-believer, towards new horizons while awaiting the last navigation, beyond the borders of Arda, towards 'true immortality'.

Afterword

Oronzo Cilli
*Winner of the Best Book – Tolkien Society Awards 2020
and Finalist of the Mythopoeic Awards – Inklings Studies 2021*

For several years, many Italian scholars have been making an essential and decisive contribution to the international debate on J.R.R. Tolkien and his works. This book written by Ivano Sassanelli falls into this broader context of relationships between Italy, the United Kingdom and the international academic and literary world.

Actually, in *The Gospel of Gollum* there are many voices that are heard: among these, the one that resonates most is that of Sméagol, who later became 'Gollum'. Sassanelli is very good at unravelling the labyrinths of the mind of this Stoor, whose strengths and weaknesses, old friendships and new adventures are exposed.

In the pages of this book, the love and passion that the author has for Gollum, his personal events and his internal transformations, are evident. Therefore, this volume is undoubtedly one of the most important academic studies on this extraordinary character created by the Professor.

For these reasons, *The Gospel of Gollum* qualifies as a valid tool for inspiration and comparison between Tolkien's works and what was subsequently produced through different media such as, for example: the two trilogies *The Hobbit* and *The Lord of the Rings* by Peter Jackson; the gameplay of *The Lord of the Rings: Gollum*; and the movie *The Hunt for Gollum* directed by Andy Serkis. Actually, in this context, it should be noted that Sassanelli dedicated a beautiful and in-depth part of his book to Andy Serkis and Francesco Vairano (the Italian voice actor for Gollum).

Bibliography

Brennan Croft J. (ed.), 2007, *Tolkien and Shakespeare. Essays on Shared Themes and Language*, Jefferson-London: McFerland & Company.

Bracco M., 2016, *Sulla distanza. L'esperienza della vicinanza e della lontananza nelle relazioni umane*, Bologna: Diogene Multimedia.

Casagrande C., 2022, *Friendship in The Lord of the Rings*, translated by Eduardo Boheme, Edinburgh: Luna Press Publishing.

Christensen B., 2003, Gollum's Character Transformation in *The Hobbit*, *A Tolkien Compass*, Chicago and La Salle: Open Court, pp. 7-26.

Christie E.J., 2013, Sméagol and Déagol: Secrecy, History, and Ethical Subjectivity in Tolkien's World, *Mythlore. A Journel of J.R.R. Tolkien, C.S. Lewis, Charles Williams, and Mythopoeic Literature*, 3(31), pp. 83-101.

Cilli O., 2016, *Tolkien e l'Italia*, Rimini: Il Cerchio.

Cilli O., 2019, *Tolkien's Library: an annoteted Checklist*, Edinburgh: Luna Press Publishing.

Coutras L., 2016, *Tolkien's Theology of Beauty. Majesty, Splendor, and Trascendence in Middle-earth*, London: Palgrave Macmillan.

da Susa E., *Summa aurea*, lib. V, *de dispensationibus*, Lyon 1537, fol. 289rb.

Di Scala R., 1999, Gollum tra alti e bassi: luci e ombre del viaggio nel male, *Endóre*, 1(1), pp. 1-5.

Fascina V., 2021, "Avanti e in alto. Insieme": percorsi Tolkieniani d'inizio secolo, in "*Vive in fondo alle cose la freschezza più cara*". *Percorsi umani, letterari e filosofici nella Terra di Mezzo di Tolkien*, Roma: Aracne, pp. 71-89.

Flieger V., 1981, Frodo and Aragorn, the Concept of the Hero, *Tolkien, New Critical Perspectives*, The University Press of Kentucky, pp. 40-62.

Flieger V., 2002, *Splintered Light. Logos and Language in Tolkien's World*, Kent: The Kent State University Press.

Flieger V., 2012, *Green Suns and Faërie: Essays on Tolkien*, Kent: The Kent State University Press.

Flieger V., 2014, The Jewels, the Stone, the Ring, and the Making of Meaning, *Tolkien in the New Century. Essays in Honor of Tom Shippey*, Jefferson: McFarland & Company, pp. 65-77.

Francis, 2016, Apostolic Letter *Misericordia et misera*, *Acta Apostolicae Sedis*, 108(12), pp. 1311-1327.

Giorgianni S., 2015, Il doppio tra Tolkien e Dostoevskij. Viaggio nella parte oscura della natura umana, *Tolkien e i classici*, Torino: Effatà Editrice, pp. 163-168.

Halsall M.J., 2020, *Creation and Beauty in Tolkien's Catholic Vision. A Study in the Influence of Neoplatonism in J.R.R. Tolkien's Philosophy of Life as "Being and Gift"*, Eugene: PICKWICK Publications.

Hopkins L., 2007, Gollum and Caliban. Evolution and Design, *Tolkien and Shakespeare. Essays on Shared Themes and Language*, Jefferson-London: McFerland & Company, pp. 281-293.

Keim C., 2007, Of Two Minds. Gollum and Othello, *Tolkien and Shakespeare. Essays on Shared Themes and Language*, Jefferson-London: McFerland & Company, pp. 294-312.

Kisor Y., 2014, "Poor Sméagol": Gollum as Exile in *The Lord of the Rings*, *Tolkien in the New Century. Essays in Honor of Tom Shippey*, Jefferson: McFarland & Company, pp. 153-168.

Mereghetti A. – Sassanelli I. (edd.), 2021, *"Vive in fondo alle cose la freschezza più cara". Percorsi umani, letterari e filosofici nella Terra di Mezzo di Tolkien*, Roma: Aracne.

Monda A., 2008, *L'Anello e la Croce. Significato teologico de Il Signore degli Anelli*, Soveria Mannelli: Rubbettino.

Monda A., 2013, *A proposito degli hobbit*, Soveria Mannelli: Rubbettino.

Monda A., 2021, *J.R.R. Tolkien. L'imprevedibilità del bene*, Milano: Ares.

Opreanu L., 2011, The inescapable other-identity transitions and mutations in the construction of Tolkien's Gollum/Sméagol, *University of Bucharest Review*, n.s. 1(1), pp. 151-159.

Paul VI, 2016, Misericordia, *Istituto Paolo VI – Notiziario*, 71, p. 7

Pezzini G., 2019, The Lords of the West: Cloaking, Freedom and the Divine Narrative in Tolkien's Poetics, *Journal of Inklings Studies*, 9(2), pp. 115-153.

Sassanelli I., 2018, *Cristo e la solitudine di Dio e dell'essere umano*, Bari: Cacucci.

Sassanelli I., 2023a, 'Who is Eru?. Literary, ethical and theological reflections about God and Religion in Tolkien's Middle-earth', *Religion in Fantasy and Science Fiction*, Edinburgh: Luna Press Publishing, pp. 1-19.

Sassanelli I., 2023b, Religious and Catholic: Primary and Secondary World in Tolkien's Letter no. 142, *Tolkien and the Relation between Sub-creation and Reality*, in *Inklings Studies Supplement*, vol. 3, 2023, pp. 107-127.

Serkis A., 2003, *Gollum: How We Made Movie Magic*, Boston: Houghton Mifflin Company.

Shippey T., 2004, Another Road to Middle-earth: Jackson's Movie Trilogy, *Understanding the Lord of the Rings*, Boston: Houghton Mifflin, pp. 233-254.

Shippey T., 2005, *The Road to Middle-earth*, London: HarperCollinsPublishers.

Testi C.A., 2018, *Pagan Saints in Middle-earth*, Zurich and Jena: Walking Tree Publishers.

Tolkien J.R.R., 1975, Guide to the Names in *The Lord of the Rings*, *A Tolkien Compass: Including J.R.R. Tolkien's Guide to the Names in The Lord of the Rings*, La Salle: Open Court, pp. 153-201.

Tolkien J.R.R., 2005, *The Lord of the Rings*, London: HarperCollinsPublishers.

Tolkien J.R.R., 2006a, Beowulf: the Monsters and the Critics, *The Monsters and the Critics and other essays*, London: HarperCollinsPublishers. pp. 5-48.

Tolkien J.R.R., 2006b, On Fairy-Stories, *The Monsters and the Critics and other essays*, London: HarperCollinsPublishers, pp. 109-161.

Tolkien J.R.R., 2006c, *The Letters of J.R.R. Tolkien*, London: HarperCollinsPublishers.

Tolkien J.R.R., 2009, Fate and Free Will, *Tolkien Studies*, 6, pp. 183-188.

Tolkien J.R.R., 2011, *The Hobbit. Or there and back again*, London: HarperCollinsPublishers.

Tolkien J.R.R., 2017a, *Lo Hobbit annotato*, da D.A. Anderson, Milano: Bompiani-Giunti Editore.

Tolkien J.R.R., 2017b, Sauron Defeated. The end of the Third Age, *The History of Middle-earth. Part Four*, vol. IX, London: HarperCollinsPublishers.

Tolkien J.R.R., 2019. *Beowulf. Traduzione e commento con Racconto Fantastico*, Milano: Bompiani-Giunti Editore.

Thomas Aquinas, *Summa Theologiae*, I-II, q. 91, a. 3.

Toninelli M., 2023. *Al Drago Verde. Quattro chiacchiere su Tolkien*, Assisi: Cittadella Edizione.

Wendling W. and S., 2012, The Riddle of Gollum: A speculative Meditation on Tolkien's Sources, *CSL*, 43(5), pp. 1-7.

Videos

Arsenale Cinema (2015). *Francesco Vairano - Incontro su 'Lo Hobbit Day'. Arsenale Cinema.* Available at: <https://www.youtube.com/watch?v=6SfbFf2qUFk> [Accessed 17 Aug. 2024].

Associazione Culturale Sentieri Tolkieniani (2014). *'Gollum contro Tutti' - con i doppiatori Francesco Vairano e Davide Perino. Associazione Culturale Sentieri Tolkieniani.* Available at: <https://www.youtube.com/watch?v=3dPHV4Zvc3Q> [Accessed 17 Aug. 2024].

Enciclopedia del Doppiaggio (2011). *Intervista a FRANCESCO VAIRANO (2011). Enciclopedia del Doppiaggio.* Available at: <https://www.youtube.com/watch?v=BUgW5ezB6vo> [Accessed 17 Aug. 2024].

Lucca Comics & Games (2017). *[Lucca Comics & Games] Francesco Vairano: L' arte della voce. Lucca Comics & Games*. Available at: <https://www.youtube.com/watch?v=_gA_eTIftno> [Accessed 17 Aug. 2024].

www.ingramcontent.com/pod-product-compliance
Ingram Content Group UK Ltd.
Pitfield, Milton Keynes, MK11 3LW, UK
UKHW020916100625
6320UKWH00022B/376

9 781915 556554